**EVERYONE KNOWS SOMEONE
WHO'S A SHEILA LEVINE . . .**

"The urge to compare Sheila with Portnoy is irresistible . . . Portnoy's introspection and self-contempt have turned him into an egocentric caricature from whom we recoil in fascinated disgust; Sheila's human loneliness and extraordinary perseverance make us want to put our arms around her . . . Parent's book is not only funny and sad; it is also sobering, because it is true!"
—**Newsweek**

"[A] funny and frightening story . . . You'll laugh at Sheila and cry for her and the many like her!"
—**Travel**

"In the best tradition of fiction as social commentary . . . The laughs come not from the belly but from that part of the psyche that feels pain . . . This development of a woman's consciousness is beautifully traced!"
—**Chicago Sun-Times**

"Funny, sad and deadly accurate!"
—**New York Sunday News**

"A REAL CHARMER. RIGHT ON SHEILA!"
—**Library Journal**

9-7

SHEILA LEVINE IS DEAD AND LIVING IN NEW YORK

Gail Parent

FOR LAIR

*This low-priced Bantam Book
has been completely reset in a type face
designed for easy reading, and was printed
from new plates. It contains the complete
text of the original hard-cover edition.*
NOT ONE WORD HAS BEEN OMITTED.

SHEILA LEVINE IS DEAD AND LIVING IN NEW YORK
*A Bantam Book / published by arrangement with
G. P. Putnam's Sons*

PRINTING HISTORY
Putnam edition published August 1972

Bantam edition / July 1973

2nd printing . . . . July 1973	6th printing . . . . . August 1973
3rd printing . . . . July 1973	7th printing . . . . January 1974
4th printing . . . . . August 1973	8th printing . . . . July 1974
5th printing . . . . . August 1973	9th printing . . . . January 1975

14 printings through December 1977

ISBN 0-553-11698-3

Published simultaneously in the United States and Canada

Bantam Books are published by Bantam Books, Inc. Its trade-
mark, consisting of the words "Bantam Books" and the por-
trayal of a bantam, is registered in the United States Patent
Office and in other countries. Marca Registrada. Bantam
Books, Inc., 666 Fifth Avenue, New York, New York 10019.

PRINTED IN THE UNITED STATES OF AMERICA

The Facts

A FEW YEARS AGO, on the East Side of Manhattan, not far from Bloomingdale's, a man set up a business where he sold diet shakes, delicious chocolate milk shakes having only seventy-seven calories. Well, I tell you, fat young girls came from near and far and lined up around the block at lunchtime. Only seventy-seven calories and such heaven! I was one of the ones that had two for lunch every day.

Many of the girls would ask the man what was in the drink. He just smiled and said, "A secret ingredient." The girls started to doubt that the shakes had only seventy-seven calories. They formed a committee and went to City Hall (or wherever it is you go to complain). The man was investigated by the Food and Drug Commission (or whoever it is who does that sort of thing). There were more than two hundred and eighty calories in those diet shakes! How could he? "How could he lie like that?" was the cry.

I'm committing suicide. DO YOU WANT TO LIVE IN A WORLD WHERE A MAN LIES ABOUT CALORIES?

Yes, I am going to kill myself. When they find my body in my small, overpriced one-room apartment, it will be slumped over this suicide note. My father will read it and nod his head. My mother will take it to bed with her and read a little each night with a glass of warm milk, slowly massaging wrinkle cream on her hands and face. My sister will skim through, and my friends . . . my friends? No, no real friends. Sorry.

My name is (was?) Sheila Levine. *Sheila Levine?* People named Sheila Levine don't go around killing themselves. Suicide is so un-Jewish.

I lived, when I lived, at 211 East Twenty-fourth Street, formerly of East Sixty-fifth Street, formerly of West Thirteenth Street, formerly of Franklin Square, Long Island, formerly of Washington Heights. Which means there are only about a hundred thousand other Jewish girls like me. Exactly like me, all with hair that has to be straightened, noses that have to be straightened, and all looking for husbands. ALL LOOKING FOR HUSBANDS. Well, girls, all you Jewish lovelies out there, good news! The competition will be less. Sheila Levine has given up the fight. She is going to die.

Why would a nice Jewish girl do something dumb like kill herself? Why? Because I am tired. I have spent ten years of my life trying to get married, and I'm tired. I know now it's just not going to happen for me. Come on, I never had a chance.

FACT: There are one hundred and three girl babies born for every hundred boy babies born. So, you figure I'm one of the extra three girls.

FACT: Many Jewish boys, à la Portnoy, grew up hating-loving their Jewish mamas and vowing to marry a non-Jewish girl. So I'm ethnically undesirable. Flat-chested blondes are in—Jewish girls, Polish girls, Italian girls are out.

FACT: Many non-Jewish girls want to marry a Jewish boy. They are encouraged by their mothers because Jewish boys don't drink or run around and they make such good husbands. Jewish girls want to marry Jewish boys for the same reasons and because Jewish husbands let their wives have maids.

FACT: This is the age of the Jewish homosexual. More Jewish boys became fags than Jewish girls became dykes. THIS COUNTRY LOST MORE JEWISH BOYS

2

TO HOMOSEXUALITY THAN IT DID IN ANY MAJOR WAR.

FACT: There are more boys who think marriage is outmoded, passé, than there are girls with the same thoughts. Women's Lib, I hate to disappoint you, but there are few members who wouldn't give up a meeting with you for a wedding night.

FACT: New York City is now crawling with thousands of girls all looking for husbands, outnumbering the boys looking for wives.

FACT: SHEILA LEVINE AIN'T NEVER GOING TO GET MARRIED. SHE NEVER HAD A CHANCE.

So, Pop, you're saying to Mom, "So she didn't get married yet. So what was so bad about not getting married that she had to go out and do this terrible thing to herself?" (She killed herself, Pop. That was the terrible thing she did. Say it, you'll feel better.)

Come on now, be fair. You and Mom are the ones who taught me how important it is to be married.

Born: August 12, thirty years ago . . . "My, what a beautiful baby." . . . "So, it's a girl, Manny? You know what that means, you have to pay for the wedding. . . ." One day old! One day old, and they're talking about weddings.

Mom, you told a story. "I took Sheila to the doctor when she was a month old, and I was so upset because she had a tiny little scratch on her face. You know how concerned I am about faces. You know what the doctor told me? He said, 'Don't worry. Don't worry yourself, Bernice. It'll be gone by the time she gets married.'" Married? There it is again, Pop, and I was one month old!

You taught me good. You bought me dolls and little stoves and little dishes to play house with. I was the mommy; Larry Singer was the daddy. "Look at the two of them. See how nicely they play. Wouldn't it be something if they grew up and got married?" You

3

know who's talking. It's the girl's mother. You hear the word "marriage," it's always the girl's mother.

It's not only the parents' fault. I heard it everywhere. I read Dick and Jane, and they had a mommy and a daddy who were married. Noah's Ark, they came two by two. Everything comes in pairs but Sheila Levine. "What do you want to be when you grow up, Sheila?" . . . "I want to be a wife and a mommy." . . . "Good girl."

Yes, I learned at a very early age that I had better get married. A Jewish mother wants her sons out of the Army and her daughters down the aisle. From the crib we hear, "It will be the greatest day of my life when I dance at your wedding." "If only I should live to see my children married, I would die a happy woman." I tried. I tried to get married and have a king-size bed and gold towels and sterling silver service for twelve. I tried for years, and what do I have? I have my old bed from home, and towels with holes because single girls buy blouses instead of towels, and four forks— three stolen from my mother, one stolen from Sardi's.

From Four to Twenty-one, Including Loss of Virginity

At FOUR I was madly in love with Alan Hirsch, who was madly in love with Cynthia Fishman. He played doctor with me but swore he would marry her when he grew up. At age four I was already the other woman. I should have known then. But no, I had hopes.

At seven, although there was no young man on the horizon, I already had my whole wedding planned. I sat with my best friend, Ruthie, on her white bedspread with my shoes off, and with the help of Lydia Lane, paper bride doll, we worked out the big event step by step. I don't remember all of it, but I do remember that Ruthie and I would have a huge double wedding, under crossed swords at West Point. Ruthie did have a wedding; only it was under a chuppah in the West Bronx. I don't blame you, Ruthie. I don't blame you at all. Congratulations and may you live to see your daughters marry.

At fourteen I knew what marriage was all about. I no longer discussed it with Ruthie. I left Ruthie in Washington Heights along with all my beloved "baby toys" that I fought to take with me to Franklin Square. "Why take them, Sheila, you never play with them anymore." I wanted my baby toys, Mother, because I was moving to a strange place and I was scared. You let

Melissa take hers. Lydia Lane and her entire trousseau were thrown down the incinerator. An omen?

So at fourteen I sat on *my* white bedspread with my best friend, Madeline—the names were much classier in the suburbs—and together we figured it out. Marriage was having a Jewish count crazy about you. We would have a house in Manhattan and a house in London and a house in Paris and a house in Rome, and we would travel from house to house to house to house with our husbands. Madeline also got married and still lives in Franklin Square not three blocks from her mother. Are you happy, Madeline? You may not think of yourself as happy, but would you trade places with me? Your home with the fake fur toilet seat for my grave?

Am I shocking you, Mother? Are you plotzing and dying and very embarrassed that your daughter killed herself. I'm truly sorry if I have embarrassed you. You could tell the Hadassah ladies that I was murdered by a jealous lover. I wish.

By the time I arrived at Syracuse University, I had my ideas on marriage really developed. My husband would have to be creative. He could be a lawyer only if he loved the theater; a doctor, if his hobby was painting; a painter, if his hobby was making money in the stock market.

I had a lot of time to develop these ideas, mainly on Saturday nights when I sat in the dorm dateless. Yes, Mom. Yes, Dad. Dateless. I was shocked, too, Mom. You always told me I was the most beautiful thing you ever saw. I lied to you on the phone every Sunday night, when I called and reversed the charges. I made up boys' names and everything. Why did you believe me? How come you thought I was so popular? Did you really expect your darling Sheila, five four, weighing in at a hundred and fifty-seven pounds, to be Queen of the Prom?

"Look, Manny, how crazy she talks. Wasn't she a beautiful girl when she was alive?"

No, my sweet parents. I sat with the other dateless girls, some too tall, some too fat, pimples, bad breath, you name it. I sat with them all in Flint Hall, watching the datable dressing, borrowing each other's sweaters and signing out. We waved them good-bye, and then we played bridge, listened to albums and ordered the hundreds of pizzas that added to our miseries. I wonder how many of the dateless became marriedless?

Syracuse wasn't all bad. I lost my virginity there. Quick, Dad, the smelling salts! Mom is plotzing again. "My daughter, Sheila, lost her virginity?"

Yeah, Mom, I got lucky.

Diane Rifkin, a girl who lived on my floor, was going with a guy named Steve in the worst fraternity at Colgate and he asked her if she had a friend for a friend of his for Winter Weekend. Three girls in the dorm turned down the offer, but I said yes.

"Listen, I have a date for your friend." . . . "What's she like? Is she pretty?" . . . "She has an interesting face."

I went so that I wouldn't have to lie to my Mommy and my Daddy on the phone. I also went because I wanted a Winter Weekend.

Steve picked us up at the dorm. He piled our suitcases and me in the back seat of his old white Impala, and he and Diane got in front. I was the mother-in-law. All the way to Colgate, I stared out the window and tried not to notice Steve's hand up Diane's dress. Diane's hand on Steve's pants. The roads were icy. One good squeeze from Diane, and dear Lord, we could have been killed.

My date was waiting for us at the fraternity house. Will Fisher. Mom, I told you his name was Will Fishman. I lied to make you happy. Were you happy?

Will Fisher was very tall and very thin. He wore

flannel shirts like the ones my mother forced me to take to camp. And he had ugly teeth. What did I expect? What did he expect?

We all went to the basketball game on Friday night and sat in the stands with the rest of the fraternity and their dates. Colgate won. I was so happy. Why? I wasn't crazy about basketball. Colgate meant little to me, and I didn't like Will. I was happy because I wasn't sitting in the dorm, playing bridge and eating pizza.

After the game, Steve, Diane, Will and I went to a small Italian restaurant—Mama Something. Cheap food, red and white checked plastic tablecloths, hard benches, Chianti bottles with candles. We bought a bottle of cheap wine and went back to the cheap apartment that the boys shared. I didn't want to go.

"Sheila, darling, listen to Mother. Don't let a boy touch you, you know where."

I had to go, Mom. I was trapped. I was trapped in a small room with unmatching madras spreads, with bullfight posters on the walls, with the Kingston Trio on the hi-fi and the whole place smelling like dirty laundry.

"SHEILA, DARLING, DON'T LET A BOY TOUCH YOU, YOU KNOW WHERE."

Very soon after we arrived at this bachelor pad (*Playboy* should have done a spread on it. I'm sure the stained walls would have come out fabulously in the photographs) the lights went out, and Diane and Steve got right to it. For half the night, there was a symphony of sounds, unzipping, unhooking, breathing, sighing, panting, the mattress creaking, and guess what, folks? . . . It went so well . . . an encore. Bravo! Bravo, Diane! Bravo, Steve! You were great! I really enjoyed listening to you. A stag film for the blind.

Do you have any idea what it's like sitting on a bed with a virtual stranger whose teeth are bad and listening to fucking? All those naughty sounds falling

8

on virgin ears. What the hell do you talk about? "So, Will, tell me all about your major," and from across the room we'd hear, "Steve, don't, that hurts."

"Do you like Bergman? I think Bergman is a genius, don't you, Will?"

"Diane, come on, roll over on your side."

Will was quiet and sneaky. Several hundred times he tried to touch me you know where. I wriggled away. He wriggled toward me. There's not much wriggling you can do in a single bed. The hand tried to touch me. I moved the hand. The hand came back. His aim was pretty good, considering the room was pitch-black. I was scared. It's not that I was sexually naïve. I spent a summer being a drama counselor at Cantor's Hotel in the Catskills. Oh, the goings-on. Look, I spent a lot of nights heavy petting, okay? In high school, I necked for hours. The boy and I both went home with rashes, but this was different.

At first we were just sitting on the bed. Then Will caught me off-balance, and we were lying on the bed. I remember I was lying there in a hot red wool dress.

"So, Will, where you from?" I removed his hand.

And from across the room, "Steve, wait, let me put the pillow under me."

"Albany." The hand was back.

"Albany, that's great. One of the girls on my floor is from Albany. Rose Morrison." I removed his hand.

"I don't know a Rose Morrison." The hand was back.

Then Will got my girdle off. I know what you're thinking. How in the hell did Will get my girdle off if I didn't want him to take it off in the first place? Persistence, that's how. Little by little he rolled it down. God, it felt good to get out of that itchy thing. Yeah, I wanted it off. Let me tell you, a panty girdle is not necessarily a good chastity belt.

The girdle unrolled and off (it caught on my leg three times; the whole project took him more than half an hour), Will got up and went to the bathroom. You know how appetizing that is before sex? I had to go, too, only I was too embarrassed.

"Come on, Sheila, darling, go to the bathroom before we get in the car."

"I don't have to go."

"It's a long ride to Grandma's. You'll be sorry."

I wouldn't let him take my dress off. I held onto it like there's some law someplace that says if you do it in a hot wool dress, it doesn't count.

My hand got tired moving his hand. My mouth got tired talking. I couldn't keep up the small talk, and he couldn't keep down his desire to do what his roommate was doing.

So, finally, as the sun was beginning to rise, I, Sheila Levine, let Will Fisher touch me you know where and he did you know what. Got it up there, didn't you, Will?

So big deal. It hurt. No tiny spot of virgin blood on his madras spread or anything. So now I couldn't be sacrificed to the gods. So I was lucky that I didn't have a Will Fisher, Jr., considering neither of us bothered to stop his sperm from fertilizing my egg.

Ruthie, remember when we found out how babies are made? We were sick. We couldn't imagine how anyone could do it, especially our own parents. Did you ever do it, Mom?

Madeline, remember how many hours we discussed what it would be like? We really and truly thought it must be a trip to heaven—violins, waves, the whole bit. Do you think Bob and Rhoda did it when we were in high school? I think so. They spent an awful lot of time together, and she was the only girl who didn't have to have pimples removed from her yearbook picture.

Oh, God, Melissa, do you remember when I told

10

you? I was thirteen and you were eight, and I told you all about penises and vaginas and everything. You went crying to Mom.

Mom and Dad, remember the night I walked in on you? I opened the door to tell you I had decided not to sleep over at Madeline's, and there was a strange rustling of sheets. Did I catch you at it, you little devils? It was a Saturday night. Did you do it every Saturday night? Did I ruin a whole week's fun by my intrusion? No. I couldn't have. My mother would never do a dirty thing like that.

So Will Fisher had me first. Good for you, Will. You won the big prize . . . Sheila Levine's virginity. Why, you weren't even overcome by emotion. No thank-you note or anything. But I would like to say thank you to you, Will, belated as it may be. Because of you, my social life at old Syracuse blossomed. I slept with a ZBT and a Sammy in one week. Ten years ago, if you did that, word got around. My name and telephone number appeared on the bathroom wall of every fraternity house on campus. No . . . not every one . . . only the Jewish ones. I wasn't particularly religious; I had just heard awful things about uncircumcised penises . . . peni?

Have you heard? Sheila Levine is an easy lay. All you have to do is call her. You don't have to buy her a drink or take her to parties or anything. You don't even have to be seen with her in public. Just call her and lay her.

I'm glad. All that sleeping around did two good things for me. First of all, I lost a little weight.

FACT: The average sex act uses up about a hundred and fifty calories. Really, that is a fact. And you don't eat while you fuck. Therefore, the more you fuck, the less you eat. It's the best diet I've ever been on.

Second of all, all that sleeping around got me rid of

11

my sexual hang-ups. Whadda you mean, Mom, don't let a boy touch you, you know where? It feels good when they touch you, you know where.

My mother got married when she was twenty. I always knew that, but as I approached two decades, she compulsively told me the story of her courtship over and over again—while she was doing her exercises, while she was wrapping toilet paper around her head so the set wouldn't fall out. I would be opening up a can of tuna fish and she somehow related what I was doing to the fact that she got married when she was twenty.

Bernice Arnold, alias my mother, was the most beautiful girl in Washington Heights. She was a petite, dark-haired, blue-eyed beauty. A beautiful, beautiful girl. This was not only the opinion of Bernice's mother and father, and Manny Levine, the man who asked for Miss Arnold's hand at her sweet sixteen. . . . No, this was the opinion of the whole neighborhood. It was the opinion of the officials, very big men, who judged the Miss Coney Island contest in 1934. Bernice Arnold entered, and Bernice Arnold won. I look like my father, and a Miss Coney Island he isn't.

Miss Arnold could have married many men. Someone who is a very big lawyer now wanted to marry her, and even a bandleader was dying for her hand. But she played the field at night, while modeling stockings during the day. Bernice had, and still has, great legs. I have stretch marks.

At twenty, her mother told her she should get married. She, as she tells it, always listened to her mother because her mother knew best. She decided to get married, choosing my father over her many other suitors. My father is a very nice person, but why would a Miss Coney Island choose him over a bandleader?

"And so, I'm telling you, Sheila, listen to your mother, like I listened to mine. Get married while you're

12

young. It's better to find someone while you're in school. Once you get out, it gets harder and harder."

Married? Married, you say? Mother, this was your daughter, Sheila, you were talking to. I wasn't programmed for marriage. In your day, things were different. In your day, there was such a thing as an ugly bride. Everyone got married. Everyone. Thin Sharon, fat Harriet, tall Bea Finkle. I was born too late, Mom.

"SHEILA, DARLING, IT'S BETTER TO FIND SOMEONE WHILE YOU'RE IN SCHOOL. ONCE YOU GET OUT, IT GETS HARDER AND HARDER."

Now, there was an unwritten code that said if you were at the end of your sophomore year and you weren't pinned or engaged or involved, then you'd better pull out of Syracuse. We had all lived through one crop of new freshmen girls, and we were not about to live through another.

Susan Fink went out with a freshman boy when she was a sophomore, and we all snickered. She showed us all when she married that freshman boy right in front of our jealous eyes. I heard, years later, that she was divorced and remarried. That's not fair, Susan. Some of us have never had our turn. Mommy, she took two turns and I haven't even had one.

The year I was a sophomore, approximately two thousand girls transferred, mostly to New York University, home for the transferred.

I would like it known that at NYU I was no longer Campus Punchboard.

FACT: It's hard to be Campus Punchboard when you're commuting.

Here I could have a fresh start. I could be the virgin again. I played virgin several times . . . up until I was about twenty-four, when it's really sick to be pure.

Finding a man—and wasn't that why we were there, girls?—finding a man was a very difficult thing at NYU. There were hundreds of Jewish lovelies, with

13

their charm bracelets, their teased hair and their shares of AT&T, all looking for Mr. Right. And if he wasn't Mr. Right now, he would be in a few years, after a few children, a house in Scarsdale and a five-thousand-dollar wedding gift from the bride's parents.

I couldn't compete. I couldn't sit in Loeb Student Center day after day pretending to read *The Behavior Problems of the Young Child,* eyes glued to the door. ... "Excuse me, is that seat taken?" ... (moving over gracefully) "No, no, it's not." ... "I see you're reading *The Behavior Problems of the Young Child."* ... (crossing legs, throwing head back) "Yes, yes, I am." ... "Could I persuade you to put it down and come with me for a cup of coffee?" ... "Love to!" (eyelashes batting so hard, they're becoming unglued) ... It never happened to me. The only man who ever spoke to me in Loeb Student Center was the guard informing me that they would be closing soon.

So I went the artistic route. I wore pants and sweat shirts and sneakers without socks in the snow.

"Manny, I don't know why that girl doesn't catch pneumonia."

Mom, you used to beg me to put on a nice dress. Practically every night when I came home, there was another box from Klein's with a "cute little outfit" (size fourteen) in it. I made you take them back, but they kept coming. Dresses in slenderizing colors, matching skirts and sweaters, a black cocktail dress for when I went out to dinner. Out to dinner?

At NYU I set up for myself a nonphysical *ménage à trois.* "Oh, no, Sheila. You said you had changed! I mean, we thought things would be better, and now this! It's too much to bear." Calm down. Calm down, everyone.

There was me, and there was Joshua. He said he didn't have a last name, but he did. His class records

14

showed him registered as Alan Goldstein. And there was Professor Hinley of the Department of Dramatic Art in the School of Education.

Oh, God, the School of Education. I never wanted to be a teacher. Never. When Ruthie and I, or Madeline and I, or my roommate Linda and I talked for hours and hours and hours about what we wanted to be, I never mentioned teaching. Not even once. When I was a very little girl, I wanted to be a wife and mommy. Ruthie, trite as it was, wanted to be a ballerina. I think I knew even then that I could never be a ballerina. I went to dancing school for as many years as Ruthie did, but I never was able to do a cartwheel or an arabesque or even walk across the room on my toes. Five years of tap and I couldn't even shuffle off to Buffalo. So I wanted to be a wife and mommy. Why, I don't know. It seemed like a good idea at the time, and I got a lot of approval from relatives.

By the time I got to high school I had definitely decided that I didn't know what I wanted to be. Of course, I eventually wanted to get married and have children. But I was selfish. I also wanted a career.

"What are you going to major in in college, Sheila, darling?"

"Liberal arts."

"I think teaching is such a good profession for a woman. Good starting salary. Good vacations, and it's always something that a girl can fall back on. Even if you get married, it's always something you can go back to when the kids are older."

"But, Mom, I hate teaching. I hate it!"

"How do you know until you try? Do me a favor, be whatever you want to be, but also be a teacher, it wouldn't kill you. Your father doesn't have money to throw out on a college education that when you graduate you're a nothing. I wish I had something to fall back on. I couldn't earn a nickel if I had to. I don't have to, thank God, but I didn't have a father who could send me to college."

"Okay."

So there I was, saddled with a drama major and an English minor in the School of Education, where I met Joshua and Professor Hinley. The three of us drifted together because we were the stars of the drama department. Joshua was the star performer, immediately cast in all productions. Professor Hinley was the star director, directing all the main stage productions. And Sheila? Sheila was the star worker. She swept the stage and painted scenery and worked the props and pulled the curtains and at the opening night party she sang the score of *Fiorello* off-key. Why did I choose drama? Why? Probably a Marjorie Morningstar fixation. I wanted approval? The final exams were easier? Kate Smith made it. I don't know.

Joshua, Professor Hinley and I ran the drama department and did everything together. Joshua and I kept the professor in coffee and doughnuts from Chock Full o'Nuts. Professor Hinley and I kept Joshua fed and clothed. My father doesn't know it, but he practically sent Joshua (Alan Goldstein) through college. Every time I ate, he ate and I paid. Mind you, I didn't mind. Joshua was one of those people whose poverty made him more attractive. For his birthday, I bought him shirts and sweaters, charged to Manny Levine.

And Professor Hinley provided us with a resting place. I commuted from Long Island, Joshua from Brooklyn. How great to have a place to rest and escape to. The good professor gave us each a key to his West Village walk-up. The good professor also gave me a C-minus in Children's Theater 101.

Joshua, Professor Hinley and I were the first flower

16

children on earth, all loving each other. It was no easy task trying to decide which of these two charming gentlemen I would finally settle down with.

"SHEILA, DARLING, FIND SOMEONE WHILE YOU'RE IN SCHOOL. ONCE YOU'RE OUT, IT'S HARDER."

Joshua had Paul Newman eyes. That's the very first thing you noticed about him, those gorgeous Paul Newman eyes. You could die from them. Not only did he have the eyes, but great brown curly hair and—I know it's crazy and you're gonna think I have some kind of fetish—feet like Elvis Presley. That sexy. I once saw a big picture of Elvis' feet in *Life* magazine, and they were exactly like Joshua's. He was moody, but with those eyes and those feet and everything in between pretty fabulous, Joshua was going to make it. Not in the movies—we of the NYU drama department didn't think in those terms. Joshua would definitely have Broadway at his sexy feet.

He could also, if he played his cards right, have me for his wife. We would live on Central Park West in a huge old co-op. We would, of course, be photographed for *Vogue*. I pictured him in a turtleneck and me forty pounds thinner. Our friends would be artistic.

"Darling, throw something on the stove, the Bernsteins will be over for din-din."

On the other hand, Professor Hinley had a lot to say for him. Very dark eyes and a very defiant air. Not handsome exactly, but well-put-together. Corduroy jackets with elbow patches and a pipe. He didn't actually have those things, but ol' Sheila would buy them for him on birthdays and anniversaries.

Ah, yes, Hinley would make it too. Wasn't he always almost involved with some off-Broadway production. In the short time I had known him, he was practically offered three directing jobs, and as soon as he actually got one, he was going to tell off the head

17

of the department and leave teaching. We would live in a Village brownstone with high ceilings and low rent.

"Darling, throw something on the stove, Salome Jens will be over for sup-sup."

Yes, it was a problem that I pondered. Joshua or Hinley—Bernstein or Jens. I didn't want to hurt either of them. Could I have both? Wife to one, mistress to the other? So little Sheila's story gets exciting? No . . . little Sheila's story gets depressing. So what did you expect?

In the middle of my senior year, just when I was deciding which of these two great men to love, they fell in love with each other. Surprised? So was I, you betcha.

I realize now why it took me so long to realize then. It's hard to tell when a man is making it with another man. There are no lipstick stains on shirts or cigarettes. There is no lingerie accidentally left. There is no engagement ring.

So how do you tell? There are ways. Single girls, listen, so it shouldn't happen to you what happened to me. The first thing to look at is clothing. Men who are sleeping together very often borrow each other's clothing. I would see a shirt of Hinley's on Joshua, Joshua's belt on Hinley. The suede jacket was passed back and forth freely. This, better than anything else, is a sure way of knowing.

They also start talking like each other. There were a lot of "Hi ya's" and "Right's!" Instead of saying goodbye, they said "Later," but only the trained ear would be able to pick this up.

The third way of telling—and this is surefire—is albums. If two guys are friends, they usually buy the same record albums. If two guys are sleeping together, they only buy one copy of the album. Take it from Sheila. I know. The day I saw *Carnival* at Professor

Hinley's and they both called it their album, I knew. What a waste of a pair of really sexy feet.

Graduation stinks at NYU. Everyone knows that. What's to celebrate? I didn't even take a picture for the yearbook. It was depressing to think I had gone to college for four years and all I had was a diploma, no husband. My mother must have thought of it as flushing my dowry down the toilet.

No one in the drama department goes to graduation. I said good-bye to my classmates the last day of tests and haven't seen or heard from most of them since. That's some successful class in dramatic arts! I saw one of them on a commercial once, and that's about it.

Sheila Levine was planning not to attend graduation. Sheila Levine's mother made her guilty thinking such thoughts.

Tap . . . tap . . . tap. I heard my mother tapping on my bedroom door.

"Sheila, it's Mother." No kidding. I thought it was Daddy with long, pointy nails.

In she came, ready for bed, covered with moisturizers. I don't know. Maybe that stuff works. Everyone was flabbergasted when they found out she had a daughter in college. "You look like a college girl yourself," they said.

"Sheila, your father doesn't know I'm talking to you. You know he's not the type of person who expresses himself well, but he's a very emotional man. I know it would break his heart if he couldn't attend his oldest daughter's graduation."

"Okay."

Lucky man. He gets to attend his daughter's graduation *and* funeral. What a thoughtful daughter!

So I graduated on the hottest day of the year. I stood proudly, sadly, with the other graduates from the School of Education, at the Uptown Campus, a place I had never been to before, far away from where the parents sat. We never went up to get our diplomas —that would have taken four and a half days. Our names weren't even announced. All the graduating doctors said the Hippocratic Oath in unison. There was a speech about commencement being the beginning. The microphone was faulty. The whole School of Engineering sat there letting the static come through.

I was trying very hard to feel something, but all I could think about was hair. I had just had mine straightened at a place on Tenth Avenue where a lot of Negroes—Negro was the right word at the time— were supposed to go. I never saw any Negroes, but I did see a lot of nice Jewish girls with frizzy hair. I felt the waves crawling under my mortarboard, ready to peep out. That's what I thought about the whole time while my mother with her Kodak and my father with his Yashica craned their necks to see their precious daughter. As a graduation present they offered me a nose job or a fur coat. I took the fur coat with a high collar.

"Our Sheila graduated. She's going to be a teacher."

No, I'm not! No, I'm not! No, I'm not!

Mom, did you have to tell the whole world I was going to be a teacher? You said it with such pride. Ruthie, Madeline, Mom, did I ever mention the word teacher?

The minute we got home that day, Dad sat down to read the paper; my thin sister, Melissa, was picked up by a nice young man in a red Corvette; Mom put the kettle on so we'd all have tea; and I went to my room to plan the rest of my life.

MY LIFE'S PLAN:
1. Get hair straightened.
2. Get a creative job.
3. Get married, etc.

On Jobs and Apartments;
Miss Burke and Miss Melkin

"SHEILA, DARLING, LISTEN TO YOUR MOTHER. TEACHING IS ALWAYS SOMETHING YOU CAN FALL BACK ON."

The Monday after I graduated, the ink on my diploma not yet dry, I went out into the world to seek my fortune. With the New York *Times* under my arm ("I Got My Job Through the New York Times"), I headed for Manhattan on the Long Island Railroad.

Tap . . . tap . . . tap.

"Sheila, darling, I don't know why you want to knock yourself out looking for a job when you can teach, be home at three, get Christmas vacation, the whole summer off, good starting salary. Mrs. Lichtman's Cynthia has been teaching for two years, loves it. Went to Europe last summer and Puerto Rico over Easter."

"Mother, I don't want to teach. I want to do something creative."

"Creative? Excuse me, College Graduate. Excuse me for even suggesting something that isn't creative."

I wanted the type of job that *Glamour* magazine writes about—WOMEN WHO ARE DOING THINGS—Sally Harding spends most of her day in a helicopter with her handsome boss, whom she married just six days after becoming his creative assistant. The picture shows Sally, blond, thin, straight hair with a little flip on the end, in a white coat, getting into a helicopter beside her big, handsome husband-boss. They are off to buy two of the world's most expensive paintings, and Mr. Harding wouldn't think of going without little Sally. Did she get her job through the New York *Times?* Did Sally's mother nudge her to teach?

As a result of an ad in the *Times,* the first employment agency I went to was called For College Graduates Only, one flight up on West Forty-fifth. Why did I think they were waiting for me? Come right this way, Sheila. Here's your creative job, and right over there, through that door, are the reporter and photographer from *Glamour* waiting to get your fascinating story.

No, they weren't waiting for Sheila. As a matter of fact, they did their best to avoid her. In the reception area—dirty beige walls, dirty beige floor, dirty beige chairs—were eight "Sheilas" and about five young "Mannys" all with the New York *Times'* classified section under their arms, ads circled in pencil. All the girls in black sheaths. All the boys in blue cord jackets. The whole group carrying trench coats, and where was Doris Day? How come she came to New York, got off the train, some man spilled coffee on her, made her head of his advertising company, lent her his handkerchief when she cried and then married her? Is there such a big difference between Sheila Levine and Doris Day? Yes. Doris Day goes to funerals to see people buried, and Sheila Levine goes to funerals to get buried.

The receptionist at the For College Graduates Only agency gave everybody a card to fill out. Ruthie, I should have been a mommy. If I had been a mommy, I wouldn't have had to fill out that card.

"Sheila, darling, if you had gone into teaching, then you wouldn't have had to fill out that card." Tap-tap-

tap all you want on my casket, Mother. I can't hear you now.

With a ball-point pen, leaning on my patent leather pocketbook: Social Security—133-30-6165. Name—Sheila Lynn Levine. Last job held—none. Reason for leaving last job (should I leave it blank? If I didn't have a last job, I couldn't have a reason for leaving it). I squeezed in, "I never worked." Then crossed that out (card looked messy). Should I ask for another? Would the receptionist think I was stupid? How do people who work in employment agencies get their jobs? Ever think about that? Turn the card over. Skills. Should I put that I type a little? If I do, then maybe they'll send me to a job that requires some typing, and I don't want to type. I want to go buy paintings in helicopters. Skills—none. (Card looking terrific. Boy, would I like to hire this Sheila Levine. Never worked. Can't do anything. Makes messes.) Question—What type of work are you looking for? Aha! I am looking for "anything creative." Last question. Education. Aha! College Graduate, you dumb asses.

I sat and waited for my turn to be interviewed, staring at the walls, avoiding eye contact wtih anyone, hoping none of the other girls landed the job of the year before it was my turn. There was a man interviewer and a woman interviewer. I hoped and prayed for the man. I don't relate to women. Never did. The only D I ever got in college was from a woman teacher to whom I didn't relate. Next? My turn. It was the woman. Come on, Sheila, relate; don't get another D. The woman motioned for me to follow her to her office. Not actually an office—one of those make-believe offices. A partitioned cubicle. She gestured for me to sit, and I sat.

"I'm Sheila Levine. I read your ad in the classified section," taking out paper, making a mess of paper all over this lady's desk. She wasn't looking at me. She was looking at my card. I bet that card really wowed her. "Ah, yes. Here it is. Brght. gal, coll. grad. good py. For College Grads Only Agency, 555-7826, 44 West 45 . . . you see, it's right here." She didn't look up. The bitch wouldn't look up and face me.

Miss Burke was the name of this charming woman. Miss Burke, whom do you think you were fooling? Your name used to be Burkowitz, and when you graduated from college, your parents offered you a nose job or a fur coat and you took the nose job, didn't you, Miss Burke? We all know that's what you did. Do you know, Miss Burke, how many people said, "That's a nose job if I've ever seen one," behind your back? Silly Miss Burke, you should have worn the nose of your heritage proudly, like Barbra Streisand and Sheila Levine.

Miss Burke made me sit in her cubicle, small, sloppy, with nebbish ashtrays, unfunny signs on the wall, like PLAN AHEAD, a big poster of Mona Lisa winking. She probably had a pencil holder in the shape of a penis in her top drawer. She made me sit there for about ten minutes without looking at me. Maybe I had her old nose. Finally she spoke. The speaking gave her away for the Burkowitz she really was. With her dress from Henri Bendel and her ten rings from Saks, her voice still said East Flatbush. Miss Burke, let me give you a piece of advice—hock the rings and take speech lessons.

"Do you type?"

"Actually I don't really want a job where I have to type. I want to do something creative. I'm here to answer your ad in the paper—the one where they were looking for a bright gal. That's me, a bright gal. Ha-ha-ha." To this day, I wish I could take back those ha-ha-ha's.

"May I see that paper, miss?"

"Certainly. Certainly. See, here's the ad. Bright gal. Ha-ha-ha."

She took the paper from me and in her alligator pumps, which I'm sure she wouldn't have worn had she known the alligator was becoming extinct, walked out of the room. Walking lessons she also had. I'm telling you, Miss Burke, get rid of the voice, you could land an Onassis.

She was back in a flash. Didn't even give me a chance to read anything upside down on her desk.

"I'm sorry, that job has been taken."

"Was it a good job?" Big mouth had to know.

"What's the difference? It's been taken."

"I was just curious. I mean, it's nice to know that somebody got a nice job. I mean, it's nice to know that there are nice jobs available. I mean. . . ."

"Do you type?"

"I type a little, but I don't want a job where I have to type. I want to do some creative type of work. I wouldn't even consider a job that required typing."

"How many words a minute?"

"Twenty-nine, but I don't want. . . ."

"Not too good. Shorthand?"

I should have said, "No, Miss Burke, and I feel this interview has come to an end. You and your people obviously don't understand what I'm looking for. Good day, Miss Burke. Next time get your voice fixed."

I said, "No," with my eyes on my chipped nail polish.

"Well, let's see if we have anything."

She started riffling through the cards on her desk, removing a paperweight of somebody sitting on the toilet. Charming. Absolutely charming. The phone rang. She picked it up immediately.

"Hello, Burke here."

She got out a new three-by-five card, on which she wrote down information with a pen that had an eight ball on the end of it.

"Yes, your name . . . the name of the firm . . . job requirements . . . typing? . . . Shorthand? . . . Preference to age, color, religion?"

Miss Burke, I hope you're not still doing that. Do you read the papers? You're not allowed to do that anymore. You wouldn't want to have to go to jail and eat bread and water and give up your charge accounts, would you?

"How much does the job pay? . . . You're kidding. I don't know if I can get anybody to work for such coolie wages."

She hung up the phone, turned to me with the new three-by-five card in her hand, and said without shame, "A job just came in you might be right for."

"Do you have to type?"

"Yes, your typing isn't good enough, but we'll lie a little. You go to 418 West Thirty-ninth, room 1411, ask for a Mr. Mann [Mankowitz?]. Call me after the interview. The fee is one week's salary, due the day employment starts."

She handed me the address on a slip of paper, and I walked out of the office in a daze, right through another crop of young hopefuls with their classified sections. God damn it, Doris Day never typed.

I never went to see Mr. Mann. For four weeks I went to twenty-three other employment agencies, where I met twenty-three Miss Burkes. To all of you, I would like to say a few words. Why not? . . . I'm a dying woman with a curse on my lips for you. So you didn't listen to me then. Would it kill you to listen to me now?

I hope each and every one of you ends up in hell. You should each have a little room like the boutique on the third floor of Saks, only they should be out of your size in everything. Your breasts should sag, and your hair should lose its shape. In front of each of you should be a typewriter. You should have permanent laryngitis and have to type instead of talk. You should get nothing until you type sixty words a minute, use a dictaphone and take shorthand—speedwriting doesn't count. The people who bring you your food will be college graduates in their black dresses and blue cord jackets. You will be forced to look at them, smile and say thank you. I wish you bad breath and space shoes. And one more thing—all your noses will grow back.

After four weeks of searching, I spent a week eating, and then I got a job. Not through an employment agency or the New York *Times*. I got my job through Rose Lehman's sister.

If a Jewish kid is an actor, he doesn't get an agent. He gets a job acting through Rose Lehman's sister or Abe's brother-in-law, who works in the same building as Fred Siegal, who is David Merrick's lawyer's barber. If a Jewish kid graduates from law school, he gets his job through Herman Marsh, who is in the garment business but has a brother who works on Wall Street and retains a lawyer from one of the top firms.

If a Jewish boy wants to be a hairdresser, there's a lot of crying at first, but have no fear, ladies and gentlemen. The first day on the job he will have a huge clientele. The Jewish boy's mother and aunts and friends will come from near and far just to have their hair teased by Goldie's boy or Harriet's nephew. They will set up so many regular appointments that he will soon own his own shop and not have to work for Italians and stop being a disgrace to his poor Mama and Papa, who saved for his college education and had to send all that money to the Bu-T Beauty School.

So I got my job through Rose Lehman's sister. She was friendly with a man called Danny Hirshfield, who lived next door to a man called Herman Nash, whose brother-in-law, Frank Holland, was in the children's record business. Rose Lehman's sister heard, right through her ears on the phone, that Frank Holland was expanding, owing to a Christmas hit he had where a lot of squirrels sang, and was taking on more help. Rose's sister swore to me that I wouldn't have to type, and the job started on my birthday, August 12 (I'm a Leo, but not your typical Leo), and I figured starting work on my birthday was some sort of omen and I couldn't stand the thought of facing another Miss Burke lady and if I didn't find a job soon, I would go crazy hearing about how wonderful teaching was for a girl. So I took the job even though it didn't have a chance of being written up in *Glamour*—WOMEN WHO ARE DOING THINGS—Here's fat Sheila Levine, just about to take coffee and a cheese danish to her boss, Frank Holland, whose real name is Frank Hyman, but he changed it when he left shoulder pads—he was the shoulder pad king—and went into the children's record business. It is widely known that Frank Holland-Hyman wouldn't have coffee and a danish if it wasn't brought by Sheila's own hands. The picture would show me in a tight black dress, wrinkles across the stomach, runs in the stockings, having a pretty big cheese danish myself.

The job wasn't great, but I was satisfied. My mother, however, was thrilled. Thrilled that I got a job in "show biz." I could hear her bragging to her friends on the phone. "Yeah, Sheila got a great job. She's involved with a record company. Why shouldn't she have such a good job? She majored in show business."

Bernice Arnold had her fling with the business. Somebody once told her she oughta be in pictures and he gave her his card. So it turned out he was a theatrical agent. My mother never went to see him because she was engaged to be married. To this day, she tells

28

people she gave up show business for my father. Come on!

I would like to take this opportunity to thank Rose Lehman's sister, Fran, for getting me the job. Thank you, Fran, thank you for saving me from the struggle. I wish I could have put up a thousand posters in the subways of New York—I Got My Job Through Rose Lehman's sister.

My roommate, Linda, and I decided way back in Syracuse that if we weren't married by the time we graduated, we probably would at least be engaged, and we would live together in Manhattan. Why not? Didn't Doris Day always have a precious, little two-bedroom apartment, all yellow and light blue and cuddly? Nothing pretentious—just a modest fifteen-hundred-a-month apartment in a gorgeous brownstone that poor Doris paid for with her unemployment check. The sheets and matching pajamas alone must have cost a fortune. Four years of college apiece, and Sheila Levine and Linda Minsk didn't know that Hollywood had been deceiving them all these years. We thought that if we were good girls and looked hard enough, Doris Day, when she was carried off into blissful matrimony, would sublet her place to us.

By August Linda had a job, too. She majored in art, which, like drama, prepared one for nothing. That was the trend. There was a whole crop of college girls prepared for nothing. Upon graduating, Linda put down her charcoal and mat knife for the last time and became a welfare worker for the New York Department of Welfare. She didn't get her job through Jewish connections; she just went there and applied. However, once she was in the department, her next-door neighbor's brother-in-law's friend's son did pull strings and got Linda into a good district. Mrs. Minsk didn't mind that her daughter worked for the Welfare Department so long as she didn't have to hand out welfare checks in a poor neighborhood.

Linda did try—a welfare worker with a heart. During her first three months with the department, she gave twenty-two families linoleum, arranged for end tables for another six and sent a young mother and her nine illegitimate children on a vacation to Florida. They never came back, which delighted Linda's supervisor so much that he took her for coffee at Chock Full o'Nuts and tried to grab her knees under the counter.

I planned to meet Linda under the arch in Washington Square Park. I left for Manhattan to find an apartment and start my life on a Friday morning. My mother hid behind her Sanka. My father hid behind the New York *Times*. I had done them wrong.

All the way in on the train, I kept thinking of the gay old times I was going to have in the big city. Had I but known then what I know now, I would have turned back and not looked for an apartment. I would have stayed in Franklin Square until I went loony enough to be locked up in an attic.

"No, no, children, don't go up there. Crazy Aunt Sheila is up there."

"Why is she crazy, Mama?"

"She's crazy because she didn't get married. Nobody thought she was pretty enough or nice enough to want to marry her, so she went crazy. That's all. No, no. Don't go up there, honey."

Yes siree! Had I known the facts . . . the actual facts . . . I never would have gone. Some call New York a jungle. It's not. It's a big jockstrap. It supports the men. Just look at the figures.

In New York City there are one million single girls who wear a size nine, have straight hair, and have never had a pimple. Not one of these girls is a virgin. They are all willing to go to bed with men in their studio apartments. They all read *Cosmo*'s articles on how to get married ("How to Get Married if You're Over Thirty"). They all go, keep going to parties for single people, Christmas Eve, New Year's Eve, election eve, any other eve they can think of. Some lie about their age. A few even lie and say they've been divorced, because if you've been divorced, your chances of getting married are better. True. If you've been divorced, it means somebody once loved you enough to want you always.

New York has one million girls who have charge accounts at Bloomingdale's and Saks, who buy their own jewelry. Girls who go to Tiffany's and buy themselves bracelets and rings. Yeah, and in case you think you're real special, you should know that these girls also went to college, have read *Faustus* and know Zola. And they're all gourmet cooks. Every one of them can make quiche and paella. They all use the same goddamned recipe.

And oh, how political they are. They're liberal, these girls. They march in the cold and join parties and wear buttons. They go to meetings because they believe in good causes? No, they go because they might meet a man who believes in good causes.

What, are we crazy? Are we all crazy? Don't we realize we're a business, we single girls are? There are magazines for us, special departments in stores for us. Every building that goes up in Manhattan has more than fifty percent efficiency apartments. Apartments? Nah—they're cells, without bedrooms, for the one million girls who have very little use for them.

All these girls, these hundreds of thousands of girls, follow the same pattern. They come to the Village first, sharing apartments with three, four, five girls, all looking for men, for husbands. They move to the Upper East Side with one roommate into smaller, more expensive apartments. They don't decorate. All their money is spent on clothes, for they are looking, searching, screaming for men. They end up alone. In small apartments, midtown, less expensive but still safe, buying skin creams and taking an interest in their pension plans. They buy some nice wineglasses, recover the old couch, and buy a cat. They have pots on their kitchen walls and plants on their living-room tables. And they never stop looking.

It would be wrong to say that none of them get married. Some do, god damn it! . . . Some do. Some marry the boy back home that they wouldn't even consider marrying when they left for Manhattan. A few meet a man at a party through a friend in the building. A very few . . . believe me, a very few. Fun City. Ha! New York is a struggle to survive, to be noticed, to be wanted, to be married. Reprints of these views can be obtained through Manny Levine, who will be happy to Xerox them for anyone interested.

I spotted Linda immediately under the arch at Washington Square Park. She was not hard to spot. Linda Minsk is five eleven in her stocking feet. On some people five eleven is fine. On Linda, the inches were not graceful. She was, at this point in her life, big, not statuesque. And she was awkward. Like just standing there, she made Washington Square Arch look peculiar. You know what people said about Linda? They said she had a very pretty face. And she did. Olive skin, big hazel eyes and a nose that didn't get in her way.

On this fine Friday, Linda wore her hair, dark and straight, teased on top of her head. Her lips were white, for she had applied coat after coat of the white lipstick which was so fashionable then. Her dress was a madras shirtwaist that looked too skimpy and hadn't had a chance to bleed. Her shoes, size eleven . . . red with baby heels. She carried a burlap sack for a pocketbook. As I remember it, Linda dressed like many girls who had recently graduated and had just started to work. She had changed positions but not wardrobes. It happened to the best of us. She was standing there and reading a copy of *Mad* magazine. No, Linda was not hard to spot.

We *both* showed up with the classified section from the New York *Times* and the *Village Voice,* our choices clearly marked. We were going to live in the Village even if it had to be in a basement. My sister Eileen did. Why not us?

"Hi."

"Hi."

"Boy, did my parents give me the silent treatment when I left Parsippany this morning. They're really upset that I'm leaving home. What about your mom? How'd she take it?"

"Great. No problem. Wished me luck."

"You're kidding!"

"Of course I'm kidding. She'd rather have me frozen in her stand-up freezer than have my own apartment."

"They're all the same."

"Yeah."

No, they're not all the same. I had a friend once named Cindy. She was eighteen and going out with this bum, and her parents threw her out of the house, that lucky girl.

Apartment ads are all lies. Every one of them. All pathological liars go right from mental institutions into making up classified ads.

The first apartment we went to had three lies in the ad. It said three rooms. It had one room. It said a hundred and eighty a month. It was two hundred and twenty dollars. It said 213 West Twelfth. There is no 213 West Twelfth. It was 213 East Twelfth. A recent inmate must have written that one.

We never got to the second apartment on our list. The telephone number was a lie. It said to call some number which was not a working number.

"Ha-ha, Myrtle, do you know what I did at work today?"

"No, what, Henry?"

"I made up a funny telephone number and put it in the New York *Times'* classified section."

"Ha-ha. That's a good one, Henry. What are you going to do next week?"

"Next Sunday I'm going to put in the number of Alcoholics Anonymous."

"Oh, Henry, you slay me. I hope they don't take you away to that awful institution again."

The third ad said, "Sep. bedroom." There was no sep bedroom to be found anywhere.

We looked at every available brownstone in our price range. There were two. Awful places. Four flights up and in the back, one flight down below the street. No windows, no air. Horrible places.

The worst part about looking at a brownstone is that you have to get the super to show it to you.

"Good morning, my friend and I have come to see about the apartment."

"So?" the sweaty super says.

"Is it possible . . . to see it? . . . If it's all right with you . . . we wouldn't want to put you to any trouble or anything." I was much nicer to this man than I've ever been to my own mother.

And with hate in his eyes and sweat all over, he beckoned us to follow him up narrow stairs, down narrow halls. He unlocked the door, threw open the closets and stood there. No high-pressure salesman, he. He knows he's got two girls dying to live in the Village.

The place was so dark and dirty we couldn't see a thing. Linda and I were scared to say we didn't like it,

34

and we were scared to confer in front of him. Finally, I got the courage to tell him we'd think about it, and he was furious. Why didn't we just leave him alone, let him drink his beer and watch his quiz show? There were bugs on the floor. I'm glad he didn't rape us.

After not finding the brownstone, we went to the Van Gogh, the Rembrandt, the Salvador Dali Arms, all new buildings with prints in the lobby. Despite the fact that they were offering one month's concession or a free mink stole, they were too expensive. They were too small. They had no charm. Doris Day got charm for her money.

Talk about shlepping. We saw every apartment in the Village and surrounding the Village. Our bones were tired, we had blisters on our feet. Toilets, toilets everywhere and not a place to go. I had to go to the bathroom all day. We must have looked at more than twenty bathrooms, and I could never bring myself to ask.

One apartment will remain in my mind forever. (Even after I'm gone. Is there a life after death? Will I still be single? Oh, boy.) The ad read, "Jr. three, East Vllg., 280 East Third, $160." Lies . . . all lies. What they considered the East Village, even the East Village wouldn't have. The apartment was in the center of the Lower East Side, which, if you want to think about it, is very funny. My father's mother and father came to this country from Rumania and lived on the Lower East Side. They worked hard—he was a tailor, worked on fur coats. As soon as they could, they moved to Washington Heights, a much nicer part of the city in those days. My father, as soon as his baby hat business was flourishing, moved his family to Long Island, and Sheila Levine, as soon as she could, was looking at apartments in the East Village, which is, face it, New Yorkers, the Lower East Side. The Levines had come full circle.

Back to the apartment. The whole goddamn thing was alcoves. There were no rooms, just alcoves. There was a sleeping alcove and an eating alcove and a sitting alcove and, I swear on my life, there was a bathroom alcove. We didn't exactly love it, but it was the end of the day and we were tired, and a hundred and sixty dollars was what we wanted to pay. So we took it.

I must admit we were pushed into it by a very strong rental agent, a Miss Melkin, who was an older version of Miss Burke, the employment agent. She kept raving about those alcoves like you've never heard.

"Here it is, girls. Don't you just love it? You can do amazing things with those alcoves . . . this is one of my favorite apartments and only a hundred and sixty dollars. I was so shocked when they told me the price. I don't know how much looking you've done, but take it from me, I've been around. You won't find anything like this for this price at this location. And with only a two-year lease. I couldn't believe it. Most apartments require a three- or four-year lease, and I've heard some of them even want five years, which I think is ridiculous, but they're getting away with it. Look at that alcove over there. Isn't it charming? You could do so much with this place with curtains. Do you realize how few apartments have a window in the kitchen alcove? This is just the type of apartment I'd like for myself if I didn't have one. I have the lease right here . . . if you girls would just sign here and give me the first month's rent, the last month's rent and a month's security, the apartment will be yours, and you can move into it tomorrow if you'd like."

Boo on you, Miss Melkin. You took unfair advantage of young girls with checkbooks. Boo on you for your fast talking and your high-pressure selling. Did you ever stop and ask yourself, Miss Melkin, "What have I done that's good for this world?" That Friday afternoon, you used your experienced mouth against two naïve maids from the suburbs. Boo! Boo on you, Miss Melkin.

We signed the lease, paid the rent and security and went back to our respective homes, a little depressed about all those alcoves. My mama met me at the door.

"So?"

"We found a place. It's really great. It has these darling little alcoves."

"Is that why you're moving? We don't have alcoves?"

"Mom, please."

"Where is this new home of yours?"

"The Village."

"Where in the Village? What's the address?"

"What's the difference? You don't know the Village."

"I have some idea. Your father and I used to go down there to look at the bohemians. Do you think you're the only one who's ever heard of the Village? I was in the Village looking at the weirdos before you were born."

"It's on East Third Street, and it has these darling alcoves that we could put curtains up on. . . ."

"East Third Street? Where on East Third?"

(Oh, boy!)

"280 East Third Street, and each little alcove can be separate. . . ."

My mother didn't get hysterical crying, like I expected her to. She got hysterical laughing.

"Manny, Manny, come here. Guess what? Guess where Sheila found an apartment, ha-ha-ha. 280 East Third. Isn't that right across the street from where your mother and father, may they rest in peace, lived when they first came to this country, ha-ha-ha?"

My father thought it was pretty funny, too. He thought it was just hilarious. The two of them really had a good time laughing at what their shmucky daughter Sheila did.

"How much?" my father speaks.

"One sixty a month, including utilities." That sobered the two of them up.

"Are you crazy? Are you nuts? My parents, may they rest in peace, lived across the street and paid twenty-seven fifty for two bedrooms and thought it was a lot."

"Daddy, that was almost forty years ago. Prices have gone up."

"It's ridiculous. I paid, for two bedrooms in Washington Heights, eighty-five a month."

"Do you really want to live in New York, where young, beautiful girls like you are murdered? And it's so dirty." I don't know which she worried more about, the dirt or the murders.

"It's a fun neighborhood."

"Getting murdered is fun?"

"I signed a lease."

"You signed a lease? You *signed* a lease? Your father will get Hyman Silverman to get you out of it. If anyone can get you out of a lease, Hyman Silverman can. He's the top attorney in the country. The best."

"I don't want Hyman Silverman to get me out of the lease. I like the place. It has all these alcoves. You should see it."

"I did see it. Your grandmother and grandfather used to live there."

"Mom, please. I'm twenty-one years old. I should be able to decide where I'm going to live."

"Listen here, College Graduate, you think you're so smart. Twenty-one is just a baby. You listen to your mother. You're not too old for me to tell you what's good and what's not good. You let Hyman Silverman get you out of the lease and you'll thank me for the rest of your life." I'm not thanking you, Mom.

Knock ... knock ... knock. ...

Who is it? My mother tap ... tap ... tapped, she didn't knock ... knock ... knock. My sister was out in a red Corvette. My father was aknocking on my door.

"Sheila? It's Dad."

I threw on my robe. The man who diapered me should not see me in my nightgown now.

"Come in."

He comes in. He is wearing the one sport outfit he owns. You have your gray Hush Puppies; you have your short black socks. You have your iridescent green pants, belted over a protruding belly. You have your shirt with the penguin, and you have the light blue hat with the air vents topping it off. A picture. Right out of *Gentlemen's Quarterly*.

Neither one of us could say anything. We'd said so little to each other over the years. I knew Will Fisher better than I knew this man standing by my window.

I didn't know him because we never talked. He talked at me and always in cliches. Like he was always telling me to be good to my feet and they would be good to me. And I never knew what to say to him. My father is so middle-of-the-road, so middle everything. Our house isn't too big and isn't too small. His business isn't too big and isn't too small. And I'll bet his you-know-what isn't too big and isn't too small.

Dad, why were you there to talk to me? You hadn't talked to me in twenty-one years. And the only plausible answer is the old joke ... "I didn't talk to you for twenty-one years because everything has been fine up to now."

I used to be jealous of all those kids in weekly television series because they talked to their fathers. Whenever there was a problem, no matter how small, a kid could have a problem with a shoelace, he would go to his father and talk about it.

39

He spoke, "Sheila?"

I was on the verge of tears. My father always did that to me. Remember when I was five, I wanted to marry you, Dad? My Oedipus complex. Electra complex? Why didn't you marry me, Dad? "Why can't I marry you, Daddy?" . . . "Because I'm already married, Sheila." . . . "When I grow up, I'm going to marry you . . ." "Give Daddy a big kiss."

"Sheila? I'm talking to you."

"Sorry."

"Your mother is very upset."

"I'm sorry she's upset. I don't know what she's so upset about."

"Your mother loves you. She wants the best for you." Aha! The two, my good man, do not necessarily follow.

"I love her, too. All I want is to pick out my own apartment. Is that so terrible? Everyone else picks out their own apartment."

"I'm not interested in everybody else. I'm interested in you." (Like when I was fifteen: "But, Daddy, everyone flunked the test. The whole class flunked." . . . "I'm not interested in everyone else. I'm interested in you.")

"If you were really interested in me, you'd let me live where I want to live."

"I can't stop you. You're a big girl. I just wanted you to know how I feel." You lied . . . you said Mother sent you. You wanted to come.

"Dad, I like the apartment. I'm sorry."

"Do me one favor. In the telephone book, list yourself as S. Levine. You never know with the nuts in the city. There are men who call up girls and say dirty words over the phone. So listen to your father and say S. Levine. That way they don't know whether you're a man or a woman." They know, Dad. Only girls with frantic fathers list their initials in the directory.

40

He leaves. Now I got guilt up to here. I got mother guilt and father guilt and guilt for wishing I was an orphan. "No, no . . . you can't leave the orphanage. You're only twenty-one."

The next morning.

Ring . . . ring . . . ri. . . .

"Hello."

"Hello, Sheil?"

"Yeah, Linda?"

"Yeah."

Pause . . . pause . . . pause. . . .

"Sheil, my mother is all upset. She doesn't like the neighborhood we're moving into." There is a grin on my mother's face. Mom, how did you know? I'm a dying woman, tell me how you knew.

"Yeah. I know what you mean."

"My father has this friend, Harry Lipschutz, who is supposed to be the top attorney in the country, who can get us out of the lease."

"What should we do?" What a question. What could we do with two mothers with two lawyers, both the top attorneys in the country, breathing down our necks?

"I don't know. What do you want to do?"

"I don't know." I don't know because nobody's ever asked me that question. "Were you so crazy about that place?"

"No. All those alcoves. What did it mean?" It meant your freedom. Freedom to make a decision. That's what it meant, Linda.

"I wasn't so crazy about it either."

Oh, Linda, why weren't you strong? Why wasn't I strong? If I had moved into that apartment, my whole life might have been different. For one thing, it might have been longer.

And so it came to pass that the two wishy-washy Jewish maids allowed their strong mothers and the greatest lawyers in the country to get them out of the lease. The two mothers then set out to find the proper dwelling for the two princess-daughters. A dwelling that would befit them. Something air-conditioned with knights in shining armor (known as doormen) at the gates to protect the maidens' virtue.

But alas, alack. The kingdom was poor. The two princesses could not afford to pay for the beautiful castle that the mothers had found. The mothers promised to give them money from their own castlehold expenses, but the princesses said, "No, we must do it on our own. We must find another princess to share the expenses." They looked all over the kingdom for many days and could not find another princess. Just as they were about to give up, a fairy godmother (you remember Joshua from NYU) appeared before them.

"I have found you a roomie!" he said. And so it came to pass the two daughters planned to move into 25 West Thirteenth Street, known throughout the land as the Mont Parnasse, with Kate Johnston, an Episcopalian. The End.

Let me tell you about Kate Johnston. I speak freely because I know that Kate will never read this. "Kate?" . . . "Yes?" . . . "Sheila Levine killed herself. She wrote this whole long suicide note telling why she did it. I know you knew her, Kate. Would you like to read her last words?" . . . "Nah."

Kate Johnston was a girl in the NYU drama department when I was there. She wore dirty underwear, and that's not my opinion—everyone in the department saw it. Never let it be said that Sheila ruined a reputation on her deathbed.

I never liked Kate. She walked into a room and made everyone in the room embarrassed for being there. She got a C as a final grade and went in to talk to the professor who gave it to her, cried a little and came out with a B-minus. She got the lead in

Streetcar Named Desire and walked off the stage because she couldn't stand the unprofessional behavior of the rest of the cast and had the director begging her to come back despite the fact that she was a rotten actress. While the rest of us were going to camp, Kate Johnston was in summer stock. And to top it all off, her parents were divorced and her father had remarried and her mother had remarried and she was the only child among them and all four of them left her alone.

So I always hated Kate Johnston. So I was jealous. So I was happy when she left school in her junior year because I thought I would never have to see her again. So? So isn't it ironic that I ended up living with the bitch? Yes, it's ironic, but you didn't have to live with her—I had to. I *had* to. We needed a third.

Halloween and Other Problems

WE OPEN on the exterior of 1650 Broadway, a dirty old building. Pan down to Sheila Levine. She is in a size fourteen black sheath, which is a little too tight so that if one looks closely with the inquiring eye of the camera, one can see exactly where her panty girdle ends. The shot should not be too tight because Miss Levine neglected to shave under her arms this morning. Sheila, about to go into the building, trips and falls to the sidewalk, ripping her right stocking at the knee and drawing blood. Miss Levine covers her knee with her pocketbook and walks hunchbacked to the closest Schrafft's, a restaurant famous for its ladies' rooms

She hobbles into the ladies' room. Close-up of knee. Close-up of Sheila's upset face. Close-up of mascara and other makeup running down Sheila's face. She washes the knee with paper towels, praying no one comes in to use the john. She removes the one torn stocking, looks at her legs and decides it is best to remove both stockings. With no stockings to hold it down, her panty girdle rolls up her fat thighs, cutting off her circulation. She puts her shoes back on, which feel terrible without stockings, throws the bad stocking away, puts the good stocking in her bag and heads back to 1650 Broadway.

Smash cut to the office where Mr. Frank Holland, a chubby, lovable type, welcomes her to the organization and tells her the squirrels hope to have not one, not two, but three big hits this Christmas. Mr. Holland takes Sheila Levine to meet Mrs. Cox, her boss-lady. On the way through the office, actually a lot of little gray offices with a lot of gray metal desks, Sheila notices that not one young man works for Frank Holland. Mrs. Cox, a middle-aged woman with dyed black hair and white boots, welcomes her and asks her if she can type. Zoom in. A very depressed Sheila simply says, "Yes."

Well, movie lovers, there it is. *The Sheila Levine Story*. The critics loved it.

I saw *The Sheila Levine Story* last night. Never have I seen a movie that thrusts one so deeply into the blues of depression. I have often been faced by a purplish despair, but usually somewhere there is a rose to lift one into a pinkish sunset. Not so with *The Sheila Levine Story*. It is deep, deep blue to the very end. The part of Sheila Levine was played by Ernest Borgnine.

Nothing Doris Day, nothing Sandra Dee, nothing Natalie Wood was happening for me or Linda or Kate. And when things don't happen in New York, you've gotta make them happen.

FACT: Girls who are in love don't give parties. Girls who are looking for love are carting out the chips and dips whenever they can.

"You know what we should do? Have a Halloween party," Kate said, standing before us nude, flicking ashes onto the green nine-by-twelve rug we all had chipped in for (and only I vacuumed).

"Good idea."

"That's a great idea."

"I love it."

"When's Halloween?"

"The thirty-first."

"I mean what day? How far off?"

"About three weeks. It falls on a Saturday."

"Perfect. That's perfect."

"We'll have it Saturday night."

(Me) "What'll we serve? I guess we should have some deli and franks and chopped liver."

(Kate) "You throw a few bowls of potato chips around. What's with the chopped liver?"

(Me) "You can't just have potato chips. What if people get hungry?"

(Linda) "Why don't we have some potato chips and some deli?"

(Me) "You can't just have some deli. You either have to have enough deli or no deli at all."

(Kate) "Potato chips and fuck off."

TO A HALLOWEEN PARTY
WHY DON'T YOU COME?
YOU WILL HAVE LOTS OF
FUN, FUN, FUN!

At the house of:	Where?
Sheila Levine	*25 West 13th St.*
Linda Minsk	*The Mont Parnasse*
Kate Johnston	*Apt. 14 L*

When? Saturday night, October 31—8:30
B.Y.O.B.

I mimeographed the invitations at the office when Mrs. Cox was in the ladies' room repairing her face. All the invitations to girls were sent exactly as you see it above. All invitations to boys had the words—*Bring Your Friends* written across the bottom. We had been to too many parties where the girls outnumbered the boys five to one. It's an awful feeling to walk into a party and have the hostess sneer at you because she was hoping, when she went to the door, there would be a man on the other side. No such thing would happen Halloween night at the Mont Parnasse.

The invitations were put through the office stamp machine when Mrs. Cox was in the ladies' room fiddling with her newly pierced ears.

The night before the fest, Linda and I tried to carve a happy jack-o'-lantern face into a pumpkin that had one side bashed in. Even though there are no perfect pumpkins in Manhattan, the question remains: What do two Jewish girls know about jack-o'-lanterns? We had pumpkins at home, but they were the plastic kind, and the pumpkin pie was bought at Horn & Hardart's Retail Shop. We carried the remains of Happy Jack to the incinerator and, lo and behold, what do we see?

We saw the first man we have ever seen in the building emptying his garbage. The building was full of girls. We saw girls in twos and threes in the laundry room, in the elevators, by the mailboxes. There is something to be learned from this. If you really want to run into that dreamboat down the hall, don't go for a building with a doorman. The male of the species is strong and has muscles and doesn't care whether the building has a doorman or not. He's not even scared of being raped.

FACT: There are more men, desirable or not, in older buildings without doormen.

Therefore, imagine our surprise when we saw this sole man in the house of little women throwing out garbage.

"Mommy, tell us again how you met Daddy."

"Won't you children ever tire of hearing that story?"

"Tell us again, *please*, Mommy."

"Oh, okay. Your Aunt Linda and I were throwing away this silly looking jack-o'-lantern that we had made, and there was Daddy, throwing out his garbage. We had been living in the same building for a month and a half, and we didn't even know it. Now go to sleep, you two little rascals. Kiss. Kiss."

47

At first Linda and I both were excited about this tall, rather good-looking guy right here in our very own hallway. My excitement waned when I noticed he was throwing his garbage out in boxes. Professor Hinley had neat garbage, too. Oh, hell.

"Hi."

"Hi."

"Hi."

"My name is Linda Minsk, and this is my friend and roommate, Sheila Levine."

"I'm Charles Miller. I live in Fourteen G." He smiled so that we could see all his caps. I was right. Gay.

"Hi." That was Linda's "Hi." Why bother cultivating someone with neat garbage and caps? "We're having a little Halloweeen party tomorrow night. Why don't you stop by if you can? . . . I know it's awfully late notice, but . . . if you can. . . ."

"I'm afraid I do have plans, but if I get home early enough. . . ."

"Great. We're Fourteen L." Linda again.

" 'Bye."

"See ya."

"See ya."

Charles Miller left the incinerator room first, and we watched him walk down the hall. He really was very good-looking. Even without the caps, he would have made it.

Back in the apartment:

"Oh, Sheila, maybe he'll come."

"Calm down, Linda. He's gay, a fag, a homosexual."

"You don't know."

"Linda, Linda, Linda, when will you learn? Anybody who puts garbage in a box has got to be queer. I'll bet inside those boxes were old eyebrow pencils."

"How do you know? I'm not going to prejudge anybody, and what if he is queer . . . that doesn't mean he won't change if he meets the right girl."

Wrong, Linda! Wrong! Many a girl has devoted her life, yes, her life, to trying to change a man who preferred men into a man who preferred women. I myself, the knowledgeable Sheila, fell into that trap. Many a young lady has felt that she is the one, the one girl who can do it. It doesn't work. He can have all the analysis in the world; he can have shock treatments and your unfaltering love—he's still going to prefer his buddy from East Hampton to you. Some girls make it a habit of falling for the gay. Why? I don't know for sure. Are they afraid of men but not ready for women? Is it an ego trip—"Guess what? I met this guy, who all his life had liked men, and then he met me and I was the one girl who could set him straight."

Don't try it, Linda. Don't try it, anybody. It ain't gonna work. You're going to be friends, maybe you're going to make it in bed a couple of times, maybe you're going to marry him, but when other daddies are taking their kids to the baseball game, this daddy is sneaking off to gay bars.

The day of the party I was dry mopping the living-room floor when Linda came back from the beauty parlor, looking great. She had straight, black, shiny hair that went flip at the end. Her waves were gone, left behind at Smart-Set, while mine were getting tighter and tighter under the *shmata* on my head. Why didn't I go to the beauty parlor? I wanted to go flip, too. Interesting. Why did I put the apartment before me? A mother martyr without ever having borne a child?

The two of us decorated up a storm, black and orange crepe paper, not so artistically streaming down from lampshades, doorknobs, scotch-taped to walls. Cardboard witches and ghosts and cats with their backs up. Over the toilet (that I also cleaned) a sign that

49

read TRICK OR TREAT. Boy, oh, boy, did we think that was funny. We thought that was so funny we had to lean on the sink to keep from falling down.

Our laughter woke up Kate. Poor Kate, it was only four thirty. There was many a Saturday that Kate slept until six, seven o'clock and woke up yawning, like it was dawn.

Kate threw on her star's robe, a robe that she got on sale at Saks for $69.95 reduced, half price—turquoise, with marabou feathers to the floor—and went into the kitchen (that I alone kept clean). There she made a peanut butter sandwich—with my peanut butter and my bread. I hated that. She always stole my food, even though I spent every Friday night initialing everything I bought. I wrote S. L. on every egg, carved it into every loaf of bread. It did no good. The bitch stole my food.

"Good morning, Kate. I mean good afternoon, I mean good evening."

"Fuck off, Sheila."

"Listen, Kate, the people will be here any minute, you've got to clean up your mess in the bedroom. [Dirty bras and underpants stacked up on a chair, dirty dresses, dirty skirts, wrinkled slacks everywhere— the old Sheila Levine look in Franklin Square.] The bedroom is a mess, and it's all your stuff around."

"Fuck off, Sheila. If I wanted to live with a goddamned mother, I would have moved in with one."

From *Women's Wear Daily*

The party at Sheila Levine's was absolutely sensational. The place was decorated in a Halloween decor, the most exquisite cardboard witches and pumpkins I have ever seen or am likely to see in many a year. The food was marvelous, superb! Rarely does one get to experience Wise Brand potato chips and Lipton's onion soup dip. It was, of course, Bring Your Own Booze. How chic!

Two of the three hostesses, Sheila, or Sheil as her friends know her, and Linda Minsk, wore the same dress, a black wool sheath, which I recognized immediately from the basement collection at Ohrbach's. It was indeed the social event of the season. Sheila Levine, by the way, did not shower for the party. Isn't she the most?

... by Greta

Yes, tall Linda and fat Sheila wore the same dress. We were a vision in black sheaths and pearls, pearls which we both had received for our sweet sixteens.

"Linda, what if nobody comes?"

"It's only eight o'clock. They're not supposed to be here until eight thirty."

"Suppose there isn't enough dip? Suppose we run out, and people are still hungry?"

"We should have put RSVP on the invitations."

"Now you mention it. Why the hell didn't you mention it when we were making out the invitations?"

"I didn't think about it then."

At eight twenty-five, the doorbell rang for the first time. Linda froze. I answered the door, and there was Joshua. Our first arrival was a fag.

"Hi, Joshua."

"Hi, Sheila."

"How's everything?"

"Fine." Joshua didn't ask me anything. He never did.

"What have you been up to?" I continued.

"Nothing much." I didn't really expect him to tell me anything. Joshua didn't answer questions either. If he were going to get cigarettes and you asked him where he was going, he wouldn't tell you.

"Well, you might as well sit down. People should be arriving soon." My eyes searched his hands. He hadn't brought his own booze. How Joshua.

The doorbell. I got it. Standing there were two clean-cut guys from the Welfare Department. Linda rushed to meet them. She towered over both of them.

"Sheila, this is Larry Hellman, and this is Ralph Glazer."

"Hi."

"Hi."

"This is Joshua."

"Joshua what?"

"I don't have a last name." They handed Linda a brown paper bag with a cheap bottle of scotch.

"Here, Linda, old girl, we'll take back anything that isn't used." They meant it. Bring your own booze also meant take your own booze when the party is over.

"Why don't we all sit down?" said I. Before I could sit—the doorbell. Three boys were standing there. It was like some sort of multiplication game. This time it was the nephew of Mrs. Cox from the office and two of his friends, whom I didn't know.

"Hi, Henry."

"Hi, this is Harvey Puckett and Norman Berkowitz."

"Hi, I'm Sheila and this is Linda and Joshua and Larry and Ralph, or is it Ralph and Larry?"

"No, you were right the first time, hi."

"Hi."

"Hi."

"Hi."

"Hi."

"Hi."

Linda took their coats into the bedroom and piled them on the bed with the others. I wished I was under them. There I was alone with six men, count them, six, and feeling rotten and self-conscious.

"How's your aunt?"

"I don't know. You see her more than I do."

"How are things down at the Welfare Department?"

"Hasn't Linda been telling you what's going on?"

"You mean about the strike?"

"Yeah."

"Yeah, Linda's been telling me all about it."

"Then whadda you asking me for?" (Hurry back, Linda, please hurry back. I'm sinking.)

"How are things with you, Joshua?"

"I told you already. Fine . . ." (Help, please, somebody, help me.) The doorbell. I never in my life thought I would be praying for girls to be behind that door, but, believe me, that night I was praying for girls. Two boys, Kate's friends, looking old and seedy, like has-beens who have never made it. Oh, boy, were they scary, they were old, almost twenty-five, I imagined.

"Is Kate here?"

"Yes, won't you come in?" (Sounded just like my mother.)

"Where's Kate?"

"She'll be out in just a moment. [Shit! Why do I say things like that?] Anyone want some dip?" . . . silence. (The party is a flop; it's falling on its ass.) "Anyone want anything to drink?"

"Yeah. Whadda you got?" This was asked by one of Kate's friends. He didn't B.Y.O.B. either.

"We have some Coke, orange soda, ginger ale, root beer and some beer," I said, charming hostess style.

"What is this, some kind of kid's birthday party or something?"

He got up and went toward the kitchen, came out holding the half-empty bottle of Larry Hellman's and Ralph Glazer's scotch.

"I'll have some of this on the rocks—that is, if you have ice."

"That's Ralph's and Larry's scotch." I was scared; suppose he got mad and beat me up or something. Suppose he broke the bottle of scotch and came after me with the broken bottle. Suppose he got a stain on the rug. He went back into the kitchen, returning with a beer that he drank from the can.

Kate came on the scene, wearing a dress Mitzi Gaynor would wear for her opening number in Las Vegas. Royal blue and low-cut, pushed up in her bra to show a cleavage I had never seen before, and I had seen a lot of Kate—the girl didn't own a pair of pajamas. Cleavage right there in my living room. Kate went over to her two friends and the three of them went into their own little corner, just a-laughing and a-giggling and having a great time. Never bothered to introduce us or anything.

The doorbell. Four guys. Why? Why, dear Lord in heaven who looks down on the universe, why did you do that to Sheila Levine? Would it have been so terrible to send a couple of girls? Kate off in a corner with her two, Sheila and Linda holding court with an even dozen gentlemen around them.

The last four were friends of ours from Syracuse, four boys with acne and dandruff who hung around the girls' dorm, too insecure to ask the pretty girls out, too uninterested to ask out the homely. We all became fast friends. They were our buddies, these guys and their platonic relationships that are such goddamned bores.

From Syracuse:

"Mom, listen, I'm bringing home a few guys for the weekend."

"Boyfriends?"

"No, not boyfriends, just boy friends."

"What's the difference?"

"I can't explain it over the phone. I'll explain it when I see you."

"All right, you know your friends are always welcome here. I'll make a big pot roast. My only wish, Sheila, is you stop having boy friends and find a boyfriend."

We introduced everybody to everybody, and then we sat around like two Scarlett O'Hara's, trying to keep our men interested. It was quite embarrassing, you know. I must be some fantastic person to have lived through it.

One half hour went by, endless time between the two of us and the twelve of them.

"Seen any good shows? Read any good books lately?"

"Where are the broads?"

"They should be here any minute. I swear to God I invited them. It's only nine o'clock. Everybody knows that people usually come late to a party. [In one sentence I alienated the whole group.] Anybody want some dip?" Silence, lots and lots of silence. "Linda, could I see you for a minute in the bedroom?" We talked behind closed doors.

"What do you think we should do?"

"I don't know, Sheil, we've got a pretty angry group out there. If something doesn't happen soon, we're going to lose them all."

"They hate us."

"Keep calm, talk, show them how nice the kitchen floor looks."

The doorbell. I rushed to open it. Six girls, six of the most beautiful girls I had ever seen and I was happy to see them. Every one of them were Kate's friends, all little starlets, but thank God they arrived. The party started. The doorbell, two more girls, friends from NYU. The doorbell, three more girls. Thank you, God, for listening to my prayers, but no need to overdo it. Pretty soon it looked like your typical New York singles party, three of the ladies for every gentleman.

The party was happening. Kate was surrounded in one corner by a group of her admirers, some of them boys—my friends—that I had voluntarily brought to her. What a shmucky thing to do. Linda seemed to

55

like Mrs. Cox's nephew, and he seemed to like her. It was he, in fact, who turned out the lights at ten. I was the perfect hostess, getting drinks, making emergency dip, mopping up spills, emptying ashtrays into other ashtrays and getting really annoyed that I had let all these dirty people into my nice, clean home.

Yes, your typical party. Peter, Paul and Mary on the hi-fi, a couple necking in the shower, two crazy college grads throwing popcorn at each other. A jolly good old time. The police arrived at around eleven thirty.

"You live here?"

"Yes, sir." (What's he doing here? There's been a murder; my mother's sick; the man at the paper stand didn't see me pay for the paper and reported me. He isn't a policeman but impersonating a policeman so that he can get in here and rape me. I resemble a well-known murderess, and they think I'm her. There are minors drinking liquor. My tax return was wrong last year; I'm going to jail.)

"The neighbors are complaining, they can't sleep." (Relief)

"I'm terribly sorry, we'll keep it down, you see we're having this Halloween party." I opened the door so that he could see that we were having a party and not performing illegal operations.

"I don't care what you're having. Just keep the noise down before we have to do something about it. This is a warning."

He went. I screamed at the top of my lungs.

"QUIET DOWN, EVERYBODY! EVERYBODY QUIET DOWN. THE POLICE WERE HERE. THE POLICE!" No one heard a word I said; they continued to make noise. The rest of the night I worried that the police would be back to cart me off to jail in a paddy wagon already containing a petty thief, two prostitutes and a woman who has just murdered her mother because she wanted her to teach.

56

"It's time to dunk for apples." Nobody heard me once again, or they chose to ignore me. The apples stood idle in a big pot on the table. It was twelve thirty, and the music was louder, despite the fact that I had already turned the volume down three times. People were in pairs, talking softly, a little light necking-petting. I was carting garbage into the kitchen.

I went into the kitchen to empty some glasses with a little scotch, a little melted ice and a lot of cigarettes in them. Yech! My back was to the kitchen door.

"Hi." I heard it, a man's voice saying hi. Who was the man behind the voice?

I spun around, threw my head back, Rita Hayworth fashion, and said, "Hi." My eyes fell on a younger, fatter version of Manny Levine. Wavy hair, small eyes behind black horn-rimmed glasses sitting on the classic Jewish nose, shirt and tie, black and narrow, brown flecked sport jacket, flecks of every color of the rainbow, brown pants, with pleats no less, a belt with the initial "N" on the buckle, brown loafers and yellow socks. Here it was, folks. Everything I had left home for. Mr. and Mrs. Manny Levine cordially invite you to attend the wedding of their daughter, Sheila Lynn Levine, to "N," at Horowitz's Catering Parlor, Sunday, November 14, at 4:42 P.M. RSVP.

"Hi and who are you?"

"I'm Sheila Levine, one of the girls who lives here."

"Yeah, I figured you live here. You've been fooling around with the garbage all night."

"And who are you? I'll bet your name begins with an *N*."

"How do you know? It happens to be Norman, Norman Berkowitz. How did you know it began with an *N*?"

"I guessed."

"You're kidding. How did you know?"

"A little birdie told me."

"Really, how did you know?"

"It's on your belt buckle."

"Oh. So, do you like living in Manhattan?"

"I just adore it. There's so much to do. It is the cultural center of the world. It's so great to have all the concerts and museums and the theaters at your fingertips." (I hadn't seen a painting, heard a note of live music or seen a show since I hit town.)

"Do you like going to museums?"

"Love it. That's why I love living in Manhattan; they're all so close by."

"Would you like to go to a museum with me?" (God, what had I gotten into? I told him I liked going to museums, but he's made it so personal, Mr. Norman Berkowitz with the pleats in his pants. I wouldn't like to go to a museum with him. I am unattracted. I don't even like standing in the kitchen with him.)

"Sure." (What else could I say? I ask you. Could I say, "Sure, but please don't wear pants with pleats and have the flecks removed from your jacket?")

"How about next Saturday afternoon?" (Oh, no, he's getting specific. I am unattracted, and he's getting specific.)

"Well, next Saturday is a bit of a problem. You see, I might have to go shopping and I think I have an appointment and my boss may want me to work on Saturday because this is his busy season and my mother may come into town and I'll have to spend time with her because I see her so little since I moved to New York."

"How about a week from next Saturday?"

"Fine."

Saying "fine" to Norman was like some kind of signal. His mind went click. Since he would be seeing me a week from Saturday, he could neck with me tonight. I was dragged into the darkness of the living room. What he planned couldn't stand the lights of the kitchen. He sat me on his lap and kissed me for about half an hour until his friend wanted to go home.

"Good-bye," said Norman, the make-out man, "I'll pick you up at one a week from Saturday. What museum do you want to go to?"

"I don't know. There are so many to choose from that I never know which one to go to first."

"How about the Metropolitan?"

"Fine, I haven't been there in over a week. They must have some great, new stuff."

I opened the door to let Norman out, only to find the men in blue again at my door.

"What's the matter, officer?" I was a little shakier this time because I had been warned by New York's finest once tonight. I definitely am going to jail. I'll hire a single lawyer. He'll fall in love with me on the stand.

"The neighbors are complaining that they can't sleep because of the noise coming from this apartment. Now knock it off."

With one swift movement, he turned on his heels and marched down the hall. His policeman partner, who had remained silent the whole time, followed right behind, managing to give me a stern look, letting me know that his buddy meant business.

Most of the noise was coming from the hi-fi. I went over and pulled out the plug. Nobody made a move. A few couples split up because they were bored with just touching each other. Touching and listening to music was something else.

Two thirty. The party was thinning out, really thinning out. Some girls were leaving with guys they had met. Others were leaving alone. The guys got bare tit half the night, and now they thought it too much trouble to take the girls home to the Bronx. The girls I felt sorriest for were the girls who had come with girlfriends and were now leaving alone because their friends had found a boy to take them home. Those were the girls who were faced with a very expensive taxi fare, split no ways. Not to mention the jealousy each and every one of us has felt in this situation.

Four ten, and everyone had gone but Joshua, who asked us to let him sleep on the couch. Why not? It's so in, so now, so today, to share an apartment with a boy. We liked the idea so much that Joshua, in his dirty suede jacket, became a semi-permanent fixture on the chartreuse couch—our only good piece of furniture. It came from Linda's basement, where it was put when her mother redecorated.

The door closed, our last guest out. I couldn't face it, much as I wanted to clean, I couldn't face it. What a mess. Black and orange everything, everywhere, paper cups, cigarettes. How could they do this to me?

"It was a great party, wasn't it, Sheila? You seemed to be having a pretty good time with the guy in the jacket with the flecks in it." (She noticed. Did the flecks shine in the dark?)

"He was all right."

"Did he ask you out?"

"Yes. I'm going to the museum with him a week from Saturday. How about Henry?"

"I'm seeing him tomorrow and the next day and the next day and every day of my life." (She's in love. Oh, no, she's in love. She found someone and she's in love and I have to pretend it's wonderful and it's not wonderful at all. It's fucking lousy. I'm jealous, so jealous that my best friend has found someone to love, I could die.)

"Linda, you sound like a girl in love."

"Oh, Sheila." (She's in love. I can tell. She's putting both legs in the same pajama leg. I'm plotzing. Why didn't it happen to me? I'm six months older. I knew Henry Cox before she did. Why did I bring him to her?)

Linda fell asleep way before I did, with a goddamned smile on her face. I lay there praying that either I find someone quickly or, if that wasn't at all possible, that Linda and Henry don't make a go of it. Dear God, bring me one or take hers away.

The minute Kate fell asleep, I got up and turned off the air conditioner. I have a sinus problem, actually a postnasal drip. Linda and Kate wanted the air conditioner on all night—I did not. I wanted it on for the evening but turned off at bedtime. If it was left on all night, I would wake up at about three and hock. Linda finally gave in. Every night before we went to bed, the air conditioner was turned off. Kate would come in late—she, I imagined, was up half the night doing naughty things with boys that I wished I was doing—and turn on the air conditioner. I woke up hocking every goddamned night.

The doorbell rang. I ignored it. I couldn't fall asleep, but I was too tired to move. The doorbell again. I dragged my weary body to the door.

"Who is it?"

"Charles Miller."

"Who?" (I was whispering so that I wouldn't wake up my precious Joshua, who was sleeping beautifully on the couch.)

"Charles Miller, I live in Fourteen G. I met you with the garbage." So I opened the door. Standing there was Charles Miller and I guessed his roommate, both in full drag, wigs and nail polish and slingbacks and shaved legs and everything. Gorgeous. They were absolutely gorgeous.

"Is the party still going?"

"No, I'm sorry, everyone has left. We're all in bed." I stopped talking and I stared.

"Okay, just thought we'd check. See you around."

"Yeah, good night."

"Good night."

They walked across the hall perfectly—none of the comic steps that men usually make when they don women's shoes. I wonder if there was love before beddy-bye.

I went back into the bedroom. Linda sat up in bed. "Who was that, Sheila?"

"Your friend from Fourteen G. He was in full drag, cobra pocketbook included. Now do you believe that Charles Miller is a fag?"

"No."

"Whadda ya mean, 'no'? He was just standing at our front door with a bra on."

Norman, as promised, picked me up at one. My first date in New York as a free and independent agent, and this is who I'm going with? Oh, how I wish that I could say you can't judge a book by its cover. That is a statement, dear friends, I cannot make. Norman wore a brown jacket with flecks, and inside there was a man with flecks in his intestines.

We went to the museum as promised. Doris Day went to museums, remember? Did she ever once go with a Norman? ("Wardrobe, you asses, he wasn't supposed to wear a brown jacket with flecks. It was supposed to be a three-piece navy pinstripe.") We walked around the Metropolitan saying things like Renaissance art, Impressionistic, Expressionistic, etc., and Norman brought me home, didn't spend a dime on me, not a nickel. I used my own token for the subway both times. I didn't invite him in.

(Me) "Thank you very much. I had a very nice time."

(Norman) "I had a very nice time, too. How about next weekend?"

(Me, thinking . . .) Are you kidding? Are you serious? I never want to see you again in my entire life.

Take your flecks and go. You make the whole building look shabby.

(Me, talking) "I'd like to very much, Norman, but I really can't; next weekend I'm washing my hair."

(Norman) "How about the weekend after that?"

(Me, thinking) Get out of the lobby already. You alone could turn this luxury building into a slum.

(Me, talking) "Sorry, I'm going home to Franklin Square the weekend after next."

"I could come out there, and we could go to the park or something." (The big spender strikes again.)

(Me, no longer able to think) "Okay."

Norman lunged for my lips and gave me the most disgusting, long, wet kiss I have ever had. Kissed me right there in the hall, six o'clock in the evening. People throwing out their garbage and he's kissing me.

Oh, boy. Norman meets the Mother.

From Franklin Square:

"So, Sheila, how was your date?"

"Boring, awful, disgusting."

"Did he ask you out again?"

"Yes. I really can't stand him. He's so repulsive to me. There's something wrong with him. He's too Jewish."

"He sounds very nice. When are you going to see him again?"

"A week from Saturday; he's coming out there."

"He's coming here?" She can't believe it. It is the first time in my life that I am bringing a nice too-Jewish boy to my parents' door. The lady is in shock.

"He's coming over Saturday. We'll drive around the island or something."

"Certainly, darling, you can take my car if you want." Take the car, take my clothes, take my house, I have tears in my eyes. You've made me a happy woman. You have brought into my midst a genuine too-Jewish boy.

Listen to Sheila, never bring home a boy to meet Mother that you're not crazy about. Norman walked in the door, and it was love at first sight. Norman and my mother fell in love. Ruthie, Madeline, everybody, listen—Norman and Bernice Levine fell in love. Yeah.

"Norman, dear, can I get you anything. Why don't you take your jacket off and make yourself comfortable? Here, Norman, have a nice cold glass of juice. Sure, put your feet up. I like people to be comfortable. I think it's so interesting that you're a third-grade teacher, Norman, tell me all about it. Is it a challenge? Do all the little girls fall in love with their teacher?"

And her eyelashes were batting, and she was wearing the bra with the good uplift and in the hair her newest wiglet. There was no denying it, she was flirting with Norman Berkowitz. It was one small trip back to the days when she was Bernice Arnold.

And her affection did not go to waste. Norman fell in love with her, completely and totally.

"Mrs. Levine, your soup is just wonderful . . . Did you really decorate all by yourself? . . . I can't believe you did all the fantastic paintings in the den."

They sure were crazy about each other, those two. She invited him to dinner, and he stayed. She invited him to stay over. Fortunately, Norman couldn't stay. He had to feed his cats (Isn't that attractive?) He was invited back for the next weekend—no consulting me —just invited back. Norman graciously accepted, shook my father's hand, kissed Bernice on the cheek. I drove him to the station so that he could take the train back to Brooklyn, where he belonged. The train was coming down the track, but he managed to grab me and kiss me before jumping from the Cadillac. I smelled my mother's chopped liver on his breath.

That night. . . .

"I like Norman very much. He's a very nice boy."

"I can't stand him."

"You don't have to marry him. Just give him a chance. Don't throw out dirty water until you have clean."

"Is that what you think of him? He's dirty water?"

"No, I happen to like him very much." I'm sure you did, Miss Arnold, we saw a lot of your terrific legs that day.

Norman came out the next weekend, and I saw him the next and the next. In those days I had two bad habits. Picking my cuticles and seeing Norman Berkowitz. No other dates were coming my way, Linda was in love with Henry Cox so she wasn't much fun, and I was really beginning to believe the dirty water theory. I would decide not to see him again, and then an old girlfriend would call to tell me that she was sporting a new two-carat diamond. (Some of those, I found out later, were total two carats—a lot of little diamonds mounted together to look like one big diamond.) Two months after our first date, I decided that I would accept the proposal, wear the ring for a while, and then throw it back in his face when Mr. Right Person came along.

What can one say about sex with Norman that hasn't been said already? We did a lot of kissing and feeling, but Norman continued to protect my virginity. (I know. I know.) We necked and petted and did everything but you know what. Why did I let the shmuck touch me? I just can't say, "I'd rather not! Please don't!" Nobody believes me when I say those things. Grace Kelly says, "Please don't," and you don't go near her. Sheila Levine says, "Please don't," and you forge ahead. I have never—Doris Day will forgive me—slapped a face. There's Sheila Levine, she'll take what she can get.

The touching and feeling and kissing went on for

many months. Norman would even undress me. Then he'd touch and feel and kiss. Do you know what a thrill that was? I began reading Margaret Mead, wondering if she wrote about his particular sexual habits.

Dear Abby,
I have been seeing this boy for seven months. I can't stand him. He makes me throw up. However, I have one problem. He won't fuck me. What should I do?

WANNA-FUCK,
Franklin Square and
Manhattan

Mixed feelings. I loathed Norman, couldn't stand his guts, but I was a passionate woman with a lot of pimples. I was also having strange dreams: Norman rips off my clothes, too impatient to fuss with the buttoms. I feel his hot breath on my back, and for the first time, I am aroused. Aroused as I never was before. My entire body is screaming, "Take me . . . take me." And he does, right there on the rug. I am shocked —I never expected such joy, such ecstasy from any man. After it is over, he strokes me gently. I sigh, for I am content. Could it ever be that good again, I think?

Okay, now here's what actually happened: My parents were out. The minute they left, to go to a long movie, they informed us, Norman went to work. Same procedure every time. He started with the kissing; he went to the feeling; he undressed me; he undressed himself for some more kissing and feeling. I was going crazy from the kissing and feeling, so I started— I'll admit it. Mom, you can skip this part if you want —I became aggressive. I grabbed his you know what with a definite purpose in mind.

"Please don't!" (That was him, folks, not me. I'm surprised he didn't slap my face.)

"It's okay, Norman."

"No, it's not. I couldn't do that to you."

"It's okay." (Another little grab, not too forceful, but firm.)

"It's not okay."

"Norman, it's okay."

"It's not okay. I would never forgive myself."

"Norman, it's okay. I'm not a virgin."

"I am."

The truth. I'm telling the truth. I was, at this point, holding the penis of a virgin male on my mother's avocado green shag rug, right beside her gold crushed velvet sofa.

"You're kidding?"

"I'm not kidding. I've never done it."

"Well, why don't you do it now? Go ahead."

"I'm scared."

He's scared. I am lying there naked, begging Norman Berkowitz to screw me, and he's scared.

"There's nothing to it. Really, Norman. Norman, are you crying? [I felt sorry for him. I did. He was crying, even though he denied it. The poor guy was scared. Like a virgin.] Come on, Norman, I'll show you."

I guided him on top of me. The minute his body touched mine, spermatozoa all over the place. You figure out where, Mom.

It was a long movie, and after coffee and a few records, we tried again. We made it this time. Norman's first time. I felt like an old prostitute. He fell asleep on top of me. Do you know for one crazy minute, I felt guilty that I had taken his virginity away from him?

Europe

Fact: Girls who are having a good sex thing stay in New York. The rest want to spend their summer vacations in Europe.

Norman was dull, the job was too much typing, and my friend Madeline was getting married. I had been in New York for nine months, and it seems I just wasn't where the action was. I thought maybe things would improve if I changed the spelling of my name from Levine to Le Vine. It was Le Vine for a full thirty days, and nothing happened. I don't know. Maybe I should have changed Sheila to Sheilah.

Linda wasn't too happy in those days either. Henry Cox, she found out after all these months, had voted for Nixon instead of Kennedy.

"Linda, I don't understand. You just don't break up with somebody because he voted differently than you did."

"You don't understand, Sheil. He voted for Nixon. I could never sleep with a man who voted for Nixon. I just couldn't."

She moped for a few weeks, and then, one afternoon, Linda came home with folders of faraway lands.

"Sheil, how much do you have in the bank?"

"I don't know . . . about two hundred and forty-one dollars."

"Great! When's your vacation?"

"Mr. Holland is very nice about it. The squirrels

don't start singing until September. I have two weeks whenever, I guess."

"Great! I've got two weeks and there's a million charter flights through the NYU Alumni Association we can get and they only cost a hundred and eighty dollars round trip and you can do it on five dollars a day and I'm sure our parents will give us a little extra."

"Let's do it! But, Linda, I don't want to do it like the tourists do it, just visiting churches and museums. I really want to get to know the people."

"Me, too. I can't stand the idea of those tours that do sixteen countries in fourteen days."

"Okay. So we have two weeks. We'll just go to London, Paris and Rome."

Were we dying to see Europe? Couldn't wait to get to the Louvre? Wandering about the Appian Way? We were dying to get away from New York, and we were dying to fall in love with a French François or a real Italian Tony. Come on, we saw *Three Coins in the Fountain*. All we had to do was fly over—all the eligible men in Europe would meet us at the plane. Not that we would marry one of them. We'd come back and marry the good old American boy, like Sandra Dee always did. But why not have one crazy fling with a man who kisses your hand?

Flight 204A. Now boarding for London.

It was a very crowded airport. For every one departing, there were three to see them off. The Minsks were there, kissing and hugging Linda, saying happy and sad good-byes. My parents were there, promising me that if I didn't listen to all their instructions, I would be robbed, raped and deported.

"Sheila, don't forget only go to nice hotels and put toilet paper down on the seats."

69

"Sheila, hide your money someplace. Don't carry it with you and don't leave it in the room."

"Sheila, if you get into any trouble, go to the nearest American embassy. They'll take care of you. Remember, you're entitled. You're an American citizen. We pay enough taxes."

"What do you do if you lose all your money?"

"I go to American Express."

"What do you do if, for any reason, you need more money?"

"I wire home for more."

"What do you do if the toilet seat is dirty?"

"I go to the American embassy."

Then, as if rehearsed, my father slyly slipped away, and my mother came in close enough to whisper.

"Sheila, you know we trust you, BUT, Sheila, you are going to a foreign country, and a lot of those men over there take advantage of beautiful American girls. Don't let a foreign boy touch you, you know where."

"Mom, I don't know where you mean." She gave me a dirty look. When I left America, my mother had a dirty look on her face.

We got on the plane, Sheila and Linda—two good friends, going to see Europe together. Two girls who planned back on Thirteenth Street exactly what their vacation would be like, one in drip-dry Arnel, one looking great.

In the year we spent in New York, Linda developed taste, the kind of taste that only New York girls have. She knew how to put things together, add a scarf, throw on a belt, swing a bag over a shoulder. She knew exactly how to dress up basic black. She had not eaten, gotten model thin, and developed flair, *savoir faire*. I had put on five pounds since I "deflowered" Norman, and accessory was not part of my vocabulary. So? Linda was next to the window, and I sat in the middle. Next to me on the other side was a very quiet, always reading, work-shirt-corduroy-pants type of guy. He managed to see past me, which was not easy to do, right into Linda's eyes. They talked over my stomach.

"Is this your first trip?" (Him)

"Yeah. I'm so excited I could die." (Linda)

"Me too." (Me)

"You're going to love it. I've been going every year for the last five years, and each year I love it more." (Him)

"You've been there five times? How fantastic!" (Linda)

"Fantastic!" (Me)

"What's your name?" (Him)

"Linda. What's yours?" (Linda)

"Charles." (Charles)

"I'm Sheila." (Me, Sheila)

Do I have to tell you that when I got up to go to the bathroom, he moved over into my seat? Do I have to tell you that when we landed, Charles got his luggage and Linda's luggage and that I shlepped my own through customs and to the cab? Do I have to tell you that he suggested a small boardinghouse, very nice, very clean, very cheap, including breakfast, with adjoining rooms? Do I have to tell you that Linda and Charles skipped around town together night and day in each other's arms, their London Fogs flapping in the breeze? And do I have to tell you that I saw the Tower of London, the Palace, Parliament, Soho, Piccadilly Circus, etc., etc., etc. all by myself, alone, on a crowded bus tour? Do I have to tell you that I have a lot of strangers in my slides?

Even though I saw it alone, I was in love with London. I felt I had to live there someday. Maybe I could persuade Frank Holland to open up a branch. If not, maybe I could get a job there, in Parliament or something. Maybe the queen could use a good girl. For her, I'd type.

"Well, Miss Levine, you seem like the kind of girl we'd like to have around the palace. Do you type?"

"Yes, Your Majesty."

"Type this letter to Scotland. I own it, you know."

My biggest fear was that Charles, out of love for Linda, was going to follow us to Paris. Our last night in London, I was packing and listening to the pitter-patter of my clothes dripping dry. Linda came back, threw herself on the bed and announced it was all over.

"Why, Linda? Don't tell me he voted for Nixon."

"He voted for Kennedy. I checked that out on the first day."

"So what's wrong?"

"He didn't love *Catcher in the Rye.*"

"That's the only reason?"

"Don't you understand, Sheila? That's my favorite book. I've read it seventeen times. I could never marry someone who doesn't love Salinger. I wouldn't want that type of man to be the father of my children."

The minute I saw Paris, I knew I wanted to live there someday. The first night I thought of changing my name back to Le Vine. Why couldn't I be an American in Paris? I could go back to New York, work for one more year for Frank Holland, save all my money—I wouldn't even walk into Ohrbach's once the whole year —and then I could come back to my Paris. I'd live on Le Rive Gauche on bread and cheese and maybe an occasional hamburger from the American drug-store and wear a lot of black turtlenecks and have that gorgeous hungry look.

Sure, my mother would be opposed to it at first. She'd probably sob at the airport. But all would be forgiven once she met Jacques, my Jewish-French husband. and my beautiful Jewish-French children, Pierre and Martine, two darlings who would carry school bags and wear navy blue socks all the time.

72

My mother would be especially pleased when I introduced her to my best friend, Brigitte Bardot. (We got friendly because we both had houses in St.-Tropez and we wore the same size bikini.)

Linda hated Paris.

"Linda, how could you hate it? I never heard of such a thing. How could you hate a whole city?"

"I just don't care for it."

"It's beautiful. You have to admit it's beautiful. The Louvre, the Tuileries, the Eiffel Tower. Everywhere you look, it's a beautiful city."

"It's okay."

"Okay? I've never, ever heard anyone call Paris okay."

Well, it was obvious why Linda was in a bad mood. She had received, via the American Express office, a sixteen-page letter from Henry Cox. He apologized over and over again for voting for Nixon and now realized what a fool he'd been. Linda had no compassion for Henry Cox, thought he was even worse for not sticking to his convictions and wanted to throw the letter into the flame at the Tomb of the Unknown Soldier. We couldn't get close enough, so she threw it in a waste basket at the top of the Eiffel Tower.

On the way back to our hotel (the Montana—we found it in *Europe on Five Dollars a Day*) the night before we left Paris, two ugly Frenchmen in a Peugeot yelled a French obscenity at us. It worked like magic, lifted Linda's spirits immediately. Our last day in the City of Light, Linda smiled and took hundreds of pictures and whistled "I Love Paris" over and over again. And by the time we were on the plane to Rome, "You know, Sheil, I'd really like to live here someday. Maybe I could get my master's in fine art at the Sorbonne or something. I could live cheaply on the Left Bank, eat bread and cheese. Wouldn't it be great?"

There was trouble in Roma. First of all, I sent a

card to Norman. I hadn't heard from him and I sent a card, damn it. I have never sent a postcard to a guy that I didn't regret sending.

Dear Norm,
   Well, we're in Rome. I've had three proposals so far —from an English lord, a French duke and an Italian count. (Only kidding.) Seriously, I'd like to live in Rome someday.

                                   See ya,
                                   SHEILA

I tried to stick my hand in the mailbox to get it back.

Second of all, Linda and her latest flame were missing for hours. I get nervous whenever I think about it.

Linda and I were having a *prix fixe* dinner in a small restaurant near the hotel. It was lovely; even the air in Rome is different. I was feeling worldly and not believing that I was really there at the same time. Home was just around the corner; Linda was starting to think of welfare, and I was thinking of Frank Holland and his records. We had both decided on this trip that we were going to get new jobs the minute we returned. We were wasting ourselves. We were too good for our jobs. We had been to Europe.

"I've got to come back here soon."

"We could come back next summer."

"No, Sheila, not just vacations. I've got to live here."

"Me too. I just wrote to Norman that very same thing. If you don't want your spaghetti, I'll eat it."

Two guys we hadn't even noticed came over to the table and asked if they could join us. Did you ever notice that when two guys join two girls, the better-looking guy automatically sits with the better-looking girl?

The guys were American—Midwest no less—button-down shirts, khaki pants and everything. Linda's was

Rick something, and mine was Joe, just plain Joe. Before I realized it, Linda and Rick took off for points unknown. Joe and I, on the back on his Honda, went to a bar where a lot of American college kids go, and I realized for the first time that I was older than my date. It's frightening. I always thought of myself as very, very young. Here was Joe waving to kids in sweat shirts—Dartmouth, Rochester, Ithaca, etc. They were all talking about school in the fall. At twenty-two, I was feeling wrinkles all over my face.

"Sheila, where do you go to school?"

(Swallow; very softly) "NYU." I was nervous. Suppose someone in the group had seen me graduate?

Linda and Rick never showed up. Joe didn't seem the least bit concerned. I, of course, began to worry when we got back to the hotel and Linda wasn't there. Joe waited with me since he and Rick hadn't decided where they were going to sleep. (How can people live like that?) We sat on hard, uncomfortable chairs in the small lobby, and we waited and we waited and we waited.

Now I'll be the first to admit that I panic, that I tend to get upset for no reason at all. If your best friend in the whole world was out with a stranger in a foreign country on a motorcycle and it was three thirty in the morning, wouldn't you panic? So did I.

"Joe, I really think we should do something or call somebody or something."

"What can we do? Who can we call?" He asked the questions but remained unconcerned.

"How about the American embassy?"

"At three thirty in the morning?"

So I got up to do something—I know not what—and in walks Rick and no Linda.

"Joe, where've you been? We've been waiting for you at Mark's."

"Where's Linda?" I said.

"I never knew we were going back to Mark's. You never told me."

"Where's Linda?" I said.

"I told you. I yelled it from the bike as we were pulling away from the restaurant."

"Where's Linda?" I said.

"I didn't hear you."

"Where's Linda? Where's Linda?" I said.

"Well, come on. I've been looking all over for you. I'm exhausted, and we leave for Madrid in the morning."

"WHERE'S LINDA?" I yelled.

"Who?"

"Linda, the girl you went out with."

"I dropped her off here right after the movie."

"You're kidding! She's not here. I'm a wreck." What did these non-Jewish boys, a Rick and a Joe, know from wrecks? I'll bet both of them had real cool, flat-chested blond mothers, who didn't even get excited when they scratched their chicken pox.

"I dropped her off, and I think she went upstairs. Come on, Joe, we're leaving early, whether you're up or not."

"Good-bye, Sheila, very nice meeting you."

"Very nice to meet you. Thanks for the drink and everything. Thanks."

I went upstairs, and I sat on the bed, and I stared. No need to get excited. Linda was obviously being held by the Mafia, who wanted her to head an Italian-Jewish-American whorehouse. The American embassy . . . call the American embassy, Sheila. Poor Linda was probably lying in some dark street somewhere, too weak to move owing to terrible constipation. Call the American Embassy. Linda had been thought a spy and was now being tortured by the fascists, who thought she had secrets to tell. So, call the American embassy!

Downstairs again. I called the American embassy. They were sleeping. Suppose Italy declared war on America? The American embassy wouldn't know until morning.

The man behind the desk saw the worry in my face. *"Polizia?"*

"Yes, please, *polizia.*"

"Polizia?" (He dialed the *polizia.*)

"I don't speak Italian. Could you tell them my *amigo, mon amie."* . . . He knew what I was saying. He had seen me waiting for hours in the lobby. He spoke to the *polizia* and gave me a "be calm" signal. I smiled at him and kept smiling. That was my only way of letting him know that I appreciated what he was doing. A lot of smiles and a lot of *grazie. Grazie. Grazie. Grazie.*

The *polizia* came and I started *grazie*ing them all over the place. They spoke with the manager for a long time, laughing and hugging and having a good time while my Linda was probably tied to the Fountain de Trevi. Finally they motioned for me to come. I motioned back, "I should come?" They motioned back to me, "Yes, you shmuck, you should come." The manager said, "Go, *polizia.*"

"Ha-ha, I'm sorry I started this whole thing. I don't really want to go. I'm terribly sorry, but why don't we all go to sleep and I'll call the American embassy when they wake up, ha-ha-ha?"

That they didn't understand. I was ushered into a *polizia* car. Why did I start up with them? I, Sheila Levine, am on my way to the *polizia* station. Lucky me, I didn't go to the police station at all. I got to go to a big, bright building way downtown. Lights everywhere, people walking around like it was the middle of the day.

It looked like some big hospital to me. Were they taking me to the hospital because they thought Linda was sick? No! It wasn't a hospital. We were in a very bright, very cold room with a few people crying, a few people looking, a few other *polizia*men, a man in a lab jacket and a lot of people sleeping on tables. Wait a minute . . . hold everything . . . HELP . . . these people ain't sleeping. Little Sheila Levine from Franklin Square, Long Island, New York, was in the Roman morgue. Oh boy, was I sick. The *polizia* were pointing and asking questions and I was sick and I thought I must be sleeping because I couldn't really be going through this. I covered my eyes and took quick looks at the ex-Italians lying on the tables. Everything was very Fellini-ish. Those faces. Thank God, there were only a few women and Linda wasn't there. Okay, already, she's not here, *grazie* anyway, you can close that drawer. No, that isn't my friend. Listen, we can go. No, that's not her. Close the drawer. No, no need to open another drawer. Thanks anyway. I looked around the room. Everyone else was looking and crossing themselves, so I crossed myself too. When in Rome . . . I'm sorry, Rabbi, but how could it be a sin since crossing came after the Old Testament?

They drove me back to the hotel. It was already light, and Miss Minsk was sitting in the lobby.

"Sheila, where have you been? I've been frantic. I was going to call the police." We fell into each other's arms, crying, exhausted, relieved.

"Where were you? I was out looking for you."

"I met this guy, Gary. He's staying right here in this hotel and we talked and talked, and he voted for Kennedy and loves Salinger."

"Linda, until six o'clock?"

"I didn't realize it was so late. Sorry."

"It's all right. I got to see more of Rome."

"You'd really love to live here someday?"

"No, I'd like to die here. They have a fantastic morgue."

Flight 432 leaving fora New Yorka.

Naturally, Charles was on the flight, too, since he also took the NYU Alumni charter. He and Linda avoided each other the whole trip, which was not easy since we were, once again, assigned three across. I, of course, was in the middle once again, which made it easier for Linda and easier for Charles and harder for me.

The two weeks had gone by so fast, like a five-second dream.

"I can't believe it's over."

"We've got to go back, Sheila."

"By next year you'll probably be married. You'll come with your husband."

"Yeah." (Whadda you mean, "Yeah"? Why don't you say, "You'll probably be married too, Sheila, and come with your husband"? I'd like to know why you didn't say that.)

"We've been in the apartment a year already. I can't believe it. The time went by so fast. Remember we met the guy across the hall and you didn't think he was gay."

"You have no proof."

"Remember the Halloween party. . . ."

"All those boys came. . . ."

"And the night we locked ourselves out. . . ."

"The first night we were there. . . ."

"It's been great. A lot of fun. I'm glad I didn't get married right out of college. Look at all the things we've done—worked, had our own apartment, seen Europe."

"Yeah. I always wanted my own apartment for a year or so before I settled down. This way I know what I want. You know what I mean?"

"I know exactly what you mean. I mean, I feel as if I've lived, you know what I mean?"

"I know. Of course I know."

We were rationalizing, preparing ourselves for our second single year in Manhattan. It had been our original plan to be at least engaged by now. We had seen and heard of friend after friend who had found her man. At twenty-two, we were already telling ourselves that it wasn't too late, that things didn't work out as quickly as we expected, but that it would happen for us as it did for some. We still had a lot of single girlfriends who were still out searching. It's just that none of us expected to be searching this long.

Customs. Watches and perfumes and gloves and lace. Everything declared because I was scared. Linda brought in loads and loads of illegal clothes. My suitcase was searched, and hers was not.

Through customs, I saw my parents, and my eyes immediately searched for Norman. He wasn't there. I was disappointed. Norman was somebody to loathe, and that's better than nobody at all.

"Hi. . . ."

"Hi. . . ."

"The trip was great. I'll tell you all about it. I have a lot of slides and postcards and everything. Where's Norman?"

"He took a vacation, too. He went with his parents to Atlantic City. Come, we'll drive you into New York."

Linda came over, kissed.

"Sheila, Charles has a car here. He'll drive us into the city if you want." I could see the relief on my father's face. The man drove seventy miles a day. He was happy not to have to make the trip on a weekend.

"Charles, the one you can't stand?"

"I can't stand him, but it's a ride. This way my parents can go home over Throg's Neck."

"Okay."

So we packed the car, and Linda and Charles sat

in front, and I sat in my usual place, alone in the back. Nobody talked. We were tired and remembering and thinking about what to do next. Should we change our jobs? Should we look for something more interesting? Should I stop seeing Norman because people will think we're going together? Should I sell the fur coat and have a nose job?

We were dropped at the curb and managed to drag ourselves and our suitcases upstairs with no help from all those people we tipped last Christmas. One look at the apartment, and we knew we had been robbed.

We were more than robbed—we were ransacked. Drapes pulled from rods and sheets thrown about and toilet paper everywhere and television nowhere to be found and record player missing and footprints on lamp shades. Oh, God. Oh, no. I'm so tired. Why not rob a person when they have the energy to accept it?

"Stop crying, Linda."

"It's a mess. The whole place is a mess. Where is Kate? Where's Joshua? Thank God I had my opal ring with me. It's a goddamned, fucking mess."

"Stop crying, Linda. Who are you calling?"

"My father."

"Put down the phone, Linda. Your father will tell your mother and your mother will tell my mother and my mother will tell my father and before you know it, you'll be in Parsippany and I'll be in Franklin Square." She put down the phone, and the minute she did, it rang.

"Sheila?"

"Yes, Mom?"

"Is everything all right? I got this funny feeling that I should have driven you into the city. I had this feeling like something is wrong." The woman, I decided, was a witch. Three hundred years ago she would have been burned. Today she's psychic.

"Everything is fine. Really, Mom."

"Okay. Why don't you relax? Put on the television or the hi-fi and relax." (How did she know?)

"Okay. Good-bye."

"Come on, Linda, let's call the police. [That is what they call them in this country, isn't it? How much is a dollar worth? It's not easy being a world traveler.] They'll come over and settle everything. They've probably caught the guy already, and they have our stuff just waiting for us to pick it up." I actually believed that.

"You call, Sheila. You're great at those things." (How did I get to be great at those things? Being manless. That's how I got to learn how to talk to police and fix toilets.)

411 . . .

"Hello, Information."

"Information, I would like the number of the police department nearest to my residence, which is 25 West Thirteenth Street, the Mont Parnasse."

"Would you like to be connected? Is it an emergency?"

"I don't know."

"You don't know whether it's an emergency?"

"Wait, I'll ask my friend. Linda, is it an emergency? [She shrugged.] My friend doesn't know either. I guess it isn't an emergency."

"The number is 555-1090."

"Thank you."

555-1090.

"Hello, Twenty-eighth Precinct."

"My apartment has been robbed and. . . ."

"Yes?"

"I'd like to report it or something."

They came (Flashing badge.) "I'm Sergeant Riley, and this is Sergeant Kelly. [They've got to be kidding.] You reported a robbery?"

"Yeah, we were in Europe, and we were robbed."

"Are you a dancer?"

"No." (A dancer?)

"A lot of dancers get robbed. They give lessons in their apartments, and the students rob them."

"No, there are no dancers here."

And he asked a few questions, like our names and did I have any suspects.

"What do you want to report missing?"

"I guess the two big things are the television and the hi-fi." (I'm doing all the talking. Linda is sitting there stunned.)

"Do you have the serial numbers?"

"The television was either an Emerson or an RCA. Do you think you can find it?"

"Are you kidding, lady? You don't know the serial numbers?"

"No." (Linda's mad that I don't know.)

"You haven't got a chance in hell that you'll ever see your stuff again."

"Can't you check the pawnshops? They did that once on *Dragnet...*"

"It ain't going to show up. You've got to be crazy, lady, if you think it's going to show up."

"Thanks anyway."

"You're lucky to be alive, lady. Good night."

"*Grazie* ... I mean, thank you. We just got back from Europe." Riley and Kelly looked at me like I was crazy. I was glad I had plans to move out of the country.

The Second Year

IN CASE you thought things picked up, it is my duty to inform you that I had a pretty rotten second year in New York.

Norman snuck back into my life. I didn't think it could happen since I'd been to Europe, but it did. I returned to the comfort of having a Saturday night date and not having to diet. I now saw Norman Tuesdays, Thursdays, Saturdays and Sundays. On Tuesdays and Sundays we did anything we could so that we didn't have to talk. And on Thursdays, when Linda was studying Eastern Religions 101 at NYU, and on Saturdays, when Linda was dating Men on the Move, we fucked. I put in my diaphragm, and we fucked. What happened to the good old days of homemade ice cream and Trojans? Remember, Madeline? In all our discussions about sex how we used to talk about the guys who carried Trojans?

So I ask you when? When did it become the women's chore? Like it was the same year that pant suits came in. Here's your pant suit, but remember, if you put on the pants, the Trojans are off. I, like all the other girls, marched to my gynecologist, paid the ten dollars, got embarrassed in front of the nurse and got my protection. (Gynecologists are in the protection racket—spread it around.)

Linda went back to the Welfare Department because it was a job she could do while looking for another job. She was in love again with a guy named Ivan Lumak, hired as a lawyer by the Burn Your Draft Card Committee. He was everything in the world that Linda wanted. He was great-looking, tall (for Linda you had to be tall), blondish, green eyes, strong jaw. He was politically minded. Linda had to have someone with a social conscience. Ivan had one further attribute. He was independently wealthy. His father was the Lumak from Well-Wear Bras—a small fortune. Linda had hit it good—tall and rich. Even her mother was thrilled. "Linda is going with Well-Wear Bras," was the cry around Parsippany.

I was terribly jealous this time. I had, I'm admitting it for the first time, a crush on Ivan Well-Wear Lumak. It was hard, very hard, to see him all the time. My heart really reacted, did little skips and things. All he had to do was smile and I stood there, gasping for air. One hello from him on the phone and I was in a coma. One "How are you?" and I plotzed for twenty-four hours. Do you have any idea what torture it was, what pain? Night after night I saw them leave, arm in arm. I was like a vulture, waiting for the moment when Linda would drop him.

What do you do when you're madly and insanely in love with your best friend's beau? I tried getting him out of my mind. That didn't work. He came to see Linda a lot and I didn't go out a lot, so there I was ready to meet and greet him. I tried staying away from him. When he came, I would try and force myself to stay in my room. I couldn't stay in my room. I would accidentally pop out in full makeup and in Kate's robe with the feathers.

"Oh, excuse me. I didn't know you were here, Ivan. [pant . . . pant . . . pant] I just came out to make myself a cup of tea. I'm quite a good cook, aren't I, Linda?"

"Sheila cooks great. She makes fantastic lasagne."

(Either Linda didn't know what I was trying to do or she didn't consider me a threat.)

"Do you like lasagne, Ivan?"

"I love it."

(thump . . . thump . . . thump . . . thump. Stop, my heart.) "I'll make it for you anytime. Tomorrow if you want. How about tonight? Would you care for some lasagne tonight? I could throw some clothes on and go to the store and get the things and. . . ."

"No, thanks, Sheila. Linda made me a TV dinner, which she burned." (He kissed the hand that ruined his dinner.)

"Well, I'll be going back to my room now. I'm going to read a little Voltaire and sew my stockings. Linda, I'll make your bed if you want."

"That's okay. I'm going to mess it up again anyway."

"Well, *bon soir.*"

"Good night, Sheil."

"Good night, Sheila." Good night! He said good night. I can't bear it.

The worst thing about the whole thing was that Linda didn't like him that much. She put him down all the time.

(Undressing) "Ivan can be so boring sometimes."

(From my bed) "I know what you mean. It's terrible when people are boring. I wouldn't spend ten minutes with a boring person."

"And he's cheap. He has all that money, I know he has, and we end up eating TV dinners at his apartment."

"How awful. That's bad news. What are you going to do, Linda, stop seeing him? Drop him?" (Please!)

"I don't know. So many things he does irk me. Like he's supposed to be this fantastic liberal, but I don't think he is. I think he just likes the idea of being called liberal. You know what I think? I think he has middle-class values. That's what I think."

"You're so right. It's amazing how wrong you are for each other. I'm surprised you stayed with him this long."

"On the other hand, there's something about him that I dig."

"Really? I have the feeling that he's not as big a Salinger fan as he says he is." So all is fair in love and war, they say. I tried for several weeks to accidentally bump into him, near his office, near his apartment.

"Oh, hi, Ivan."

"Hi, Sheila, what are you doing here?"

"My dentist is around the corner. I'm on my way for my six months' checkup."

"I'm glad, so glad, I ran into you. If you only knew how much I've wanted to be with you these last few months. I kept seeing Linda just to be near you."

"Oh, Ivan."

"Shhh. Don't talk. Come, Sheila. At last. Forget the checkup. Your teeth, like the rest of you, look beautiful to me."

. . . Fantasy.

Reality. . . .

I finally met up with him in front of his building.

"Oh, hi, Ivan."

"Hi, Sheila, what are you doing in this neighborhood?"

"I come here to buy filet mignon. They have the best filet mignon in the city. [Acting like I just got a bright idea. Light bulb over my head.] Say, why don't I buy a couple of filet mignons and make one for you with a baked potato and sour cream and chives and a salad?"

"Sounds great. Wish I could, but I'm exhausted. I'm going to throw on a TV dinner and go to bed."

"Tomorrow night?"

"I just can't plan ahead."

"See ya."
"See ya around, Sheila."

Norman is such a nice boy. Okay, that's true. Only he didn't stimulate me in any way. I was, at twenty-two, not feeling old enough to settle. Not that I had a choice—there was no proposal forthcoming. For Christmas there was a wool scarf from Norman, not a sparkling diamond with a small but perfect stone. If I didn't get the ring, how was I going to throw it back in his face? How was I going to call girlfriends to tell them I had broken the engagement, canceled the wedding, when there was no wedding on the horizon?

Yeah, Norman is a nice boy, but he was bad in bed, he gave rotten gifts, and you couldn't really take him everywhere. That's not true—Norman was the type of boy you couldn't take *anywhere*. Linda's Ivan fit in anytime, all the time. Not so with Norman. January of the second year we lived in Manhattan, Kate got cast in an off-off-Broadway show. She played girl number four in a production called *Rebirth,* where she had to wear a loose black cape and a lot of white makeup and had to say a lot of "fucks" and "craps." Naturally, we were all very proud of her. And what does this have to do with Norman?

Linda and I were invited to the opening-night performance. We had to pay for our own tickets, but it was nice being invited anyway. Made us feel inside. We were also invited to the opening-night party after the play. Now an opening-night party is not exactly the place one would take a boy in a brown-flecked jacket. Here was my chance. I could go to the party without Norman—just to see how well I did without him. Probably some great guy would come up to me and we'd start talking and probably he'd take me home and he'd take my number and probably I'd start seeing him and would slowly drop Norman. I wondered if I should invite Norman to the wedding.

I invited Joshua to go with me. He wasn't hard to reach. He was now spending at least three nights a week on our couch. The other nights he was at parties. I'm not kidding. He spent most of his life at parties. I don't mean Saturday nights and special occasions. I mean four, five, six nights a week. He didn't even look for a job. There was no time. Between dressing and going to parties, there was no time for Joshua to do anything else.

So Joshua, in his beige corduroy pants, a light blue shirt and his brown suede jacket, and Sheila, in her drab green turtleneck dress and her graduation fur, and Linda, looking great, dark hair cascading down a plum sweater dress, and Ivan the beautiful, wearing I-don't-remember-what, he was so gorgeous, all took a cab and went in the dirty January snow to the Judson Memorial Church basement to see *Rebirth*.

I liked going places with Joshua. He didn't open doors or pull out chairs or hold hands, but he was a very handsome chap. It had been a long time since I had been seen with anything presentable.

Strange play. A lot of people playing a lot of symbols. One of those cerebral things where you are bored to death, but you're scared to say so because you'll be labeled stupid by a group of pseudointellectuals. Let's just say that there were lots of lines like "Earth Mother is upon us now." Kate and five other actresses and actors went slithering around the stage in bare feet and white makeup and did a lot of kneeling and yelling.

At intermission:

"I love the director's use of abrupt movement, which is in direct opposition to the smoothness of the author's lines." (Joshua)

"I feel the author is trying to tell us that there is good and evil in all men." (Sheila)

89

"Through the use of masks, which I think is brilliant, what they are actually saying is that all men are alike." (Ivan—God, he's beautiful)

"The theme seems to be brotherhood, like all of us could use the 'rebirth' or brotherhood within ourselves. If more people saw this play, the world would be a better place to live in." (Linda)

The second act of *Rebirth* was the same as the first —a lot of kneeling, makeup and yelling. The play ended with all six cast members lined up at the foot of the stage with their arms outstretched, while the lights went from green to red and back to green again and then—blackout. Applause . . . applause . . . applause. . . . The actors took serious dramatic bows—one by one. . . . Applause . . . applause. Then the actors took a bow in unison, still all very intense, no smiles, wiping their brows. Lights up, and the audience, which consisted of about twenty-four people, each one a friend or relative of one of the members of the cast, plus a couple of priests who always show up at those church productions, left quietly.

Backstage, Kate was playing star in her robe with the feathers. (Would Ivan recognize it?) Removing her makeup with her unscented Albolene cold cream, used by the stars for more than a century, she arose gracefully from her impromptu dressing table to greet us. Kate had style. There were three girls in the dressing room, which was obviously a Sunday school classroom. Kate was the only one with long-stemmed roses.

"So glad you could come." (Sounded like Julie Andrews, opening night of *Camelot*.)

The party was in a loft, the first and last loft I have ever been in. There are always rumors about lofts, like— A friend of mine has this fantastic loft facing Washington Square Park for fifty dollars a month.

Everybody was talking favorably about the play. Our

host was the director. It was not the type of party where you wait up for the reviews, for it was not the type of play that was reviewed. This is the type of play where the director keeps promising his unpaid actors that the off-Broadway critic from the New York *Times* should be down next Wednesday.

Joshua and I split up shortly after we arrived. After all, we didn't want to be competition for each other. He headed for the director. I headed for the peanuts. Linda and Ivan were talking intimately and very intensely in the corner, so that left me to sip my ginger ale, eat my peanuts and try to mingle. I got into three conversations.

Conversation number one was with a very intense, turtle-necked young man, whom I happened to find attractive. I'll admit I started conversation number one.

"Hi, so what did you think of the play? I liked it very much."

"I felt it was pretentious."

"I know what you mean."

"Overdone."

"I know what you mean."

"If I had directed it, it would have been very different. Do you know what I mean?"

"I know what you mean. Are you a director?" (He gets insulted and picks himself up.)

. . . End of conversation number one.

Conversation number two was with another single girl, from NYU's drama department, Pesha Pinkus, a ladies' handbag buyer's assistant. She started conversation number two. There is nothing worse than getting into a long conversation with a girl at a party. Every single girl knows that every minute spent talking to another girl is a wasted minute.

"Hi." (Pesha Pinkus speaking)

"Hi." (Sheila Levine here)

"So what's new?"

"Nothing much." (Sheila Levine trying to ease her way out of conversation)

"I'm working at Bonwit's and it's a ball. I can take as long as I want for lunch and. . . . [Please, how am I going to get away from this woman and mingle? MINGLE. That's the most important thing you can do at a party. That's your only chance. There's a guy over there with an empty glass. . . .] The hours are great, and my boss is really nice. She knows everything about handbags. She picked up a fake crocodile. . . . [The guy is moving. He's mingling. He's talking to another guy, thank God.]

"Excuse me, Pesha, I have to. . . ." (Pesha, please, this is so important to me. There's a guy over there.)

"Wait, let me tell you who I saw the other day. Remember Bob Lankey? I bumped into him in the subway, the BMT, maybe it was the IRT, anyway. . . . [Let me go. Let me go, Pesha!] I thought it was Bob Lankey the minute I saw him. . . . [I've *got* to mingle, Pesha, please, I don't have much time left at this party, honey.] We were laughing about the time. . . ."

"Excuse me, Pesha. . . ."

"Don't you want to know what we were laughing about?"

"No."

. . . End of conversation number two. End of Pesha's friendship. End of chance to get pocketbooks wholesale. I escaped right into conversation number three.

"Hi." (Me talking to the cute guy I spotted. I didn't just go right up to him—I carried a bowl of peanuts. The way to a man's heart is through his peanuts.)

"Hi." (A friendly smile. I plunged.)

"Did you see the play tonight?"

"No, I didn't, but my wife did." (Uh-oh. I'm not used to this. I'm young. Too young to know married people.)

"What did she think of it?" (So how do I get out of this gracefully?)

"She didn't like it. You interested in a scene?"

"What?" (I really didn't know "what." You've got to remember that I was a drama major. To a rather naïve drama major, a scene is part of a play that you perform in front of the drama department. I am now at a party where there are a lot of "theater"-oriented people, with some exceptions, like Pesha from pocketbooks. I think I am being discovered. Good-bye to Frank Holland Records. Hello, off-off-Broadway. Give my regards to off-off-Broadway?)

"A scene—you interested?"

"I guess so." (So what do I change my name to—Sheila Lee?)

"Great! My wife digs scenes." (I am confused.)

"Your wife digs scenes?" (I am embarrassed because I feel I am asking dumb questions.)

"Yeah, but she doesn't like lesbos. You a lesbo?"

. . . End of conversation number three. End of party. Joshua was bored, and Linda and Ivan had left already, so it was good-bye-I-had-a-very-nice-time time.

Why, of all the nights of my life, do I choose this one to tell? Why is this night different from all other nights? . . . It's not. That, my love, is the problem. It was your typical single girl night on the town—a date with a gay friend, a boring play. Who do you think supports off-off-Broadway? . . . The single girl.

FACT: Yentas from Long Island support Broadway, but it is the single girl, with nothing to do on a Thursday eve, who will buy a cheaper theater ticket.

What does it all add up to? Nothing. Simply nothing—a waste of a lifetime and a lot of ticket stubs. I had been thinking for the last year and a half every time I went to a party that if only I wasn't with Norman, I would meet Sheldon Right. I was without Norman,

93

and I insulted someone, got stuck with a big-mouth girl and was offered a scene. Nothing.

Oh, Madeline, Ruthie, what were you two married ladies doing that night? Having a pot roast at home, screaming at kids to get into bed, and arguing about what time to go to bed yourself, since you're a night person and he's a day person. Sounds like heaven. Did you have sex? Did you hate your husbands that night because you went to college and you've been stuck in the house with some smelly two-year-old all day, whom you adore but yelled at all afternoon? Did you wish that instead of sitting next to your husband on the gold velvet couch with the Scotchgard watching a movie on television that you were out on the town with a darling homosexual? Be fair, girls. You want your fun. You're tired, but you're in no mood for trades. You're not going to give up your man and your paneled den for ol' Sheila's life.

One week after Kate opened in *Rebirth,* she told us that she was moving in with her director. Just like that —out of our apartment—into his loft. Didn't care how she hurt us. (Sounding more like Mrs. Levine every day.)

"Why are you moving?"

"I feel like it. He asked me to live with him, and I decided to do it."

"You can't leave."

"Why not? I can do any fucking thing I want. Who's going to stop me?"

"Good-bye, Kate."

From the New York *Times*—"Two Jewish gals looking for third to share their new, modern Village apartment. $60 a month. Call 555-8342."

The ad was wrong, right? Wrong phone number. It was their fault, and we ran the ad again the following Sunday. I must admit the ad was still wrong. It should have read—in all fairness to the readers—"Two Jewish girls and Joshua, looking for fourth."

We got calls.

First call:

(Me) "Hello."

(Him) A lot of heavy breathing.

(Me) "Hello?"

(Him) "What's your cup size?" (More heavy breathing and click.)

Second call:

(Me) "Hello."

(Him) "I'd like to suck your cunt." (Click.)

A total of eight responses from Jewish girls and eight responses from perverts. The question is: Are there specialized perverts who call only Jewish girls?

Late Saturday night we got calls from girls who picked up the Sunday paper the minute it came out. We got calls bright and early Sunday morning. They all asked the same question—"How many bedrooms?" We said "one" and they said "good-bye." All those Jewish girls kept asking the question and hanging up. A couple of them came over but felt the place wasn't big enough and left.

The following Sunday from the New York *Times*— "Two Jewish girls want to share apartment with same. Beautiful but small, one bedroom. 555-8343."

More calls. This time we interviewed a bevy of beauties. Ever meet someone whom you never knew before and you might be living with? How do you find out if they're clean, cooperative and courteous? You look at the girl and if her nails are clean and she doesn't look like she's going to ruin your social life due to her long, beautiful natural blond hair, you take her in. We took in Charolette Whooper. It was a big mistake.

Charolette was clean, but not at all cooperative and courteous. Her rent was late, she made long-distance calls which she refused to pay for, and she fucked at home. Yes, Miss Whooper brought her suitors home with her, to the Mont Parnasse yet, took them to her room—which was our room—and fucked. Did it often and did it long. Linda and I and Joshua spent many long, long evenings atop the chartreuse sofa waiting for pants to be zipped and certain parties to be out the door.

Linda and I were literally kicked out of our own apartment. We had to get rid of the fucking Miss Whooper. We also had a big decision to make—our lease was up in September. How did it happen? I didn't expect to be living with Linda through one lease. Now what do I do? Linda had prospects for marriage every week. She was turning them down because they voted for Nixon or they were pro-Johnson or they were phony dressers, and there was a new one—they had no chance if they didn't die from the Beatles' third album. I was still wondering when Norman was going to pop the question so that I could spit in his eye. No luck so far.

We were a little older, a little wiser, thanks to Charolette Whooper, a lot sadder. How did this happen to us? Why were we worrying about another lease, instead of wondering what kind of attaché case to buy our husbands for Valentine's Day? We weren't exactly panicked, but we were wondering. It was happening —love and marriage were passing us by.

"We have to get rid of Charolette, Sheil."

"Our lease is up in few months anyway. Why don't we look for another place? Just for the two of us so that if one of us gets married or something, then the other one won't be in that much trouble. It'll be a lot easier finding one roommate than two."

"Yeah." (That was Joshua, who obviously had every intention of remaining on the chartreuse couch, wherever it might be.)

It was Linda who decided that we should look on

the Upper East Side because the Village was full of fags and kids. The kids were young girls, the age we were when we first moved in. I listened to Linda because Linda seemed to know things now. Actually, I listened to anyone who was thin.

So it was impossible to get back to Europe. We spent our entire vacation looking for that one bargain on the Upper East Side. Somebody always knows somebody who got this fantastic place right off Sutton Place with floor-to-ceiling windows and balconies, rent-controlled for—get this—a hundred dollars a month.

We spent twelve sweaty days looking. I alone ruined three linen dresses with sweat stains. We faced the same lies in the classified section and were beaten by the same rental ladies.

"I don't know, I'm really not sure. It's smaller than our other place and only thirty dollars less. . . ."

"It's up to you. You've probably been looking for a while. [She could tell by the condition of my armpits.] All I can say is that by the time you make up your mind the apartment will be gone."

"Okay."

To Franklin Square. . . .

"Mom, I put down a deposit on an apartment." (Mom, do something. Get me out of it. Get your best lawyer in the whole country and get me out of it and you find me a place to live.)

"So good luck. Where is it?"

"On East Seventy-seventh. It's 201 East Seventy-seventh." (Hate it, Mom, and get me out of it. PLEASE!)

"Very fancy."

"I'm not even sure I like it." (Get the lawyer.)

"You always feel that way at first. I'm sure you'll love it. For a housewarming present, your father and I want to give you a hundred dollars and I want you to buy something nice for the apartment."

I was disappointed, so disappointed, that she didn't scream and yell and get my money back. What the hell was going on?

We told Charolette we were moving. She kept the old apartment and had about six strangers move in with her. Seven people whom I didn't even know were inheriting the contact paper I had personally lined the kitchen shelves with.

We rented another U-Haul-It, and all our friends helped us move. We told our mothers not to bother coming in, and they didn't come. (Don't they love me anymore?) So I was the one who had to clean out the toilets, and Norman put the locks on the doors. I took the hundred dollars my parents gave me and bought five throw pillows, a new bedspread, curtains and an electric can opener. (That way, I could get to the food faster.)

It wasn't the same as when we moved into our first home. Linda had a date the first night. I washed my hair. No excitement. Doris Day had only one apartment in New York before she got married.

I really didn't want to work for Frank Holland forever. For many reasons. I had to type. That's reason enough. And I wasn't meeting any men on the job—a lot of squirrels, no men. I had been in New York for almost two years, and nothing was happening, baby.

I looked for work. Followed up every ad. Female, help wanted, college grad. Didn't learn my lesson and went back to employment agencies. Met a lot of new Miss Burkes and told them I didn't want to type. Even Rose Lehman's sister didn't work out. Rose had moved to a great part of Great Neck and had gotten stuck up, or so my mother said. She and my mother didn't speak very much. The only way I could get to her sister, Fran, would be to go down to Texas and try to bump into her.

I thought of going to California to see what the work situation was out there . . . "Guess what, Darryl, Sheila Levine is coming out here to look for work."

"You're kidding? We'll put her on our next picture. She can be assistant to the director and star."

I couldn't pick myself up and go. I'm not doing anything here, but I might not do anything there. My social life isn't great here, but who says it's going to be great there? My mother carried on when I went forty-five miles away. What might she do if I moved three thousand? That settles it. I'll stay. There are definitely more pros than cons. After all, would New York be Fun City without me? "I, Mayor Lindsay, would like to personally thank Sheila Levine for staying in New York. . . ."

Flashbulbs. . . . "Mayor, please, would you kiss Miss Levine again. We'd like to get another shot."

So finally a job showed up. My cousin Mindell, who travels a lot, met this writer on a boat or something and got his phone number. Mindell, who lives in Riverdale, called him one day when she was in New York and he asked her over for tea, no less. Anyway, Mindell, bless her yenta heart, mentioned that she has a very bright cousin (me, who else?), and the writer said that he was looking for someone to do research on his next book.

So cousin Mindell, who travels a lot (that's how everyone in the family refers to her—"cousin Mindell, who travels a lot"), told my mother that her Sheila should hurry and call the writer. And her Sheila did. The writer's secretary, a man (tee-hee), told me that Mr. Swernson, the writer, would see me Thursday at four. Go explain that to Mrs. Cox and a bunch of squirrels.

"Mrs. Cox, I really have to leave early on Thursday because I'm getting married."—Too phony.

"Mrs. Cox, I have to leave early on Thursday because I have to see the doctor."—Never, she'd ask questions.

"Mrs. Cox, I have to leave early on Thursday because I am looking for a new job."—Honest, but stupid.

(On Thursday) "Mrs. Cox, I woke up this morning with a terrible headache and a stomachache and a sore throat and a temperature of a hundred and four. And there are spots all over my face. And I've been throwing up and have laryngitis. My doctor will probably send me to the hospital. . . . Yes, I'll be there tomorrow."

Mr. Swernson, here I come! I come with knowledge about you and your work.

Swernson, Randolph. Born 1912. Has written more than a hundred books about travel. (My cousin Mindell travels a lot.) Some of his more famous ones are: *Spain, Land of Dreams; France, Country of Beauty; Italy, Reality and Fantasy;* and *Sweden, a Warm Country in a Cold Climate*.

On the subway there, I kept thinking (it's hard to think with all those Miss Subway candidates staring in your face—one black, one Puerto Rican, one Wasp and one nice Jewish girl)—so little Sheila has made it at last—*Cosmopolitan* Girls on the Move, *Glamour* Girls on the Go, *Vogue* People Are Talking About. . . . Yes, people are talking about Sheila Levine, co-author of Randolph's latest. Maybe not co-author, but dedicated to. . . . This book is dedicated to Sheila Levine, my love, my wife. I could not have done it without her. The dedications would grow through the years as we had children. This book is dedicated to my darling wife, Sheila Levine Swernson, and our darling children, Medea and Zacharia.

Imagine my surprise when I found out that 262 East Sixty-second is a town house. A real live New York town house, doncha know. I rang, a polite little ladylike ring.

"Miss Levine?" the short, slim male secretary (tee-hee) said.

"Yes, I'm Miss Levine," Miss Levine with pocket-book in front of missing button said.

"Please sit down," he said. "Mr. Swernson will be with you in a moment."

So do I take off the coat? When somebody says to sit down, does that mean you should take off your coat? I made several false moves and then decided to take it off. Whereupon male secretary sneaked back into the room to help me off with it. He, I am sure, saw a button was missing.

"Tsk-tsk," the male secretary must have thought. "What a slob! My love, who is a male nurse (tee-hee), would die laughing if he saw this coat."

The room I sat in was decorated rich. Yeah. Old and new rich all over the place. Antiques without a scratch. That's rich. A lot of silver things around. Little awards and leatherbound books. Not a spot on the upholstery. That's rich. And paintings with plaques. How many people do you know who have paintings with plaques? Things from all over the world. The man did a lot of shopping. "Hello, Mr. Swernson, what would you like today?" . . . "Do you have anything in a six-thousand-dollar clock? And I'll have that jade elephant. It'll look lovely next to the sterling silver cigar box from England and the Waterford vase from Dublin." The man was a shopper. You can inherit antiques, but you don't inherit upholstery without spots. Did the male secretary pick it out from a lot of swatches?

More than half an hour later the male secretary asked me to follow him upstairs to Mr. Swernson's study. He has a study. Not a study-alcove—a study. God! Suppose he dies and remembers me in his will. . . . "And to my fine friend and research assistant, I leave my green jade elephant and thirty-five million dollars."

He was at a huge desk, sitting in a huge leather wing chair. Just like in the movies. I had a bit of *déjà vu*. Who knows? Maybe in another life, I was a wealthy woman or a job applicant.

"Miss Levine, I met Mindell on my last crossing. She spoke very highly of you. [I sat and listened, didn't say a word. He wasn't handsome, forty-five, bad skin, but boy, was he impressive.] I am looking for a research assistant for my next book, *Lichtenstein, a Small Country*. I'll need someone who is creative. [That's me—I'm creative. You've found me at last.] And, of course, I need someone who can type. [Shit.] I am sure you will find the work interesting. Why don't you speak with my secretary and he will discuss all the details with you?"

I was led into another office. That's the whole interview? The secretary, Mr. Henley-Jones (what the hell's with the hyphen?), told me that I could start in two weeks and that I should report to work at four o'clock in the afternoon on October 25. And good-bye, Miss Levine, and thank you for coming.

I left so confused. Did I get the job? I think so. Did I say I would take the job? I don't think so. What is the job? Who the hell reports for work at four in the afternoon? I don't know. How much does it pay? Oh, my God, I don't know. Have no idea. Must be a lot. Look at all those antiques. Sometimes rich people are cheap. Better call Mr. Henley-hyphen-Jones. Will he think I'm dumb for asking? Should I just go? What's the difference what it pays—it's the type of work that I've been looking for. But I'm a single girl—supporting myself. I've got to know what jobs pay.

"Hello, Mr. Henley-Jones, please."

"Who is calling?"

"Miss Levine."

"One moment, please." (Does the secretary have a secretary? Does he have a Bigelow on the floor?)

"Henley-Jones here." (Don't you love it? He's probably from Oklahoma, went to fifth grade.)

"Mr. Henley-pause-Jones, I was wondering if you needed me for anything before I came to work, like I could work at night or something."

"That won't be necessary, Miss Levine."

"I don't mind, call me if you like, and also [sound casual], my accountant was wondering how much I will be making. He has to know since he takes care of all my finances. I don't have to know. He does."

"You can tell your accountant that the job pays ninety-five dollars a week, and if you'll excuse me, Miss Levine, there are matters I must attend to."

"Certainly, Mr. Henley-pause-Jones."

NINETY-FIVE A WEEK. HELL. FUCK. BITCH. SISSY. DOODY. CRAP. Three years in New York, three raises from Mr. Frank Holland. Now making a hundred and thirty-five a week. Back to ninety-five. That bitch Swernson. He has the money. I saw the antiques. Let him hock the elephant. I won't do it for ninety-five. I can't. Ninety-five is take-home sixty-five. One sixty-five for the apartment. I can't make it. I have to support myself. I'm single, you know. Frank Holland is nice, and maybe things will improve up there. There was talk about the squirrels doing a Christmas special next year. Maybe I'll be involved in that and I'll meet some people through it and I'll get into television. Oh, Christ. Back to Frank Holland and the help wanted pages.

Dear Mr. Swernson,
  I regret that I will be unable to take the position you offered me at this time. Perhaps some time in the future I will be able to work for you.
                                        Sincerely,
                                        SHEILA LEVINE

Shit.

Fire Island

OUR THIRD YEAR in New York was a flop. Linda went through several romances, all flops. Norman was a flop. Work was a flop. I was a flop. Linda's job was a flop, and Joshua, still on our couch, recovered in red corduroy, was a flop. Even the cover on the couch was a flop.

Okay, something had to be done. You just can't sit there in the midst of flop. So I brought a nice selection of wines, two twenty-five a bottle, into the apartment. I didn't hang around Linda so much because she looked too good. Just as I was about to beg *Glamour* magazine to make me a Glamour Make-Over, a miracle happened. An answer to our prayers. Our escape appeared. Charles Miller, the guy with the neat garbage from the Mont Parnasse, appeared before our very eyes and told us that for two hundred and seventy-three dollars each, we could share a house with six other people for the summer on Fire Island.

If you're wondering why Charles Miller and his roommate wanted to share a house with us, there is a simple explanation, my friend. The year before, Charles shared a house with five guys at Cherry Grove. One night his lover was stolen on the dunes. He just didn't want the competition this year and felt if he went to a straight part of the island, like Ocean Bay Park, he wouldn't have to worry about losing his lover or what he was wearing and he could relax.

Fire Island! Fire Island every other weekend, four people in a tiny house. Sounded like heaven. Fire Island was to us what Atlantic City was to our parents . . . Fire Island—America's Playground.

Were we interested, because if we were interested, we had to tell Charles right away. He already had six people in on the deal—he and his roommate; Mark Marks, a guy we had never heard of; Agatha Horowitz, a girl we had never heard of; and the Ponties, a couple who had moved into our old apartment after Charolette Whooper was evicted. Every time I saw the Ponties they had just been fighting. She always had red eyes and dripping mascara.

"I don't know, Linda, what do you think we should do? Fire Island with all those people? We hardly know them. They might be the types who like orgies and stuff. They might be messy."

"Sheila, all I know is my cousin Rhoda took a house there last summer with eleven people, and out of the eleven people, she got three proposals."

Three proposals! I would have gone up to five hundred dollars to get in on that deal. Beautiful. A house on Fire Island. Everyone is doing it, and I wouldn't have to hear, "Sheila, darling, why don't you come home this weekend? It's so hot in the city." And I could get away from Norman. So I'll lose twenty pounds, buy a flattering bathing suit, pack my reflector and go.

"Here they come, Isaac, the summer people. They come here every year and think that they can take over the place. I wish we had a law to keep them out."

"Someday we will, Maria. Be patient. Someday we will."

The house that Charles had originally arranged for fell through. The owner had a group of ruffians there last year who practically destroyed a two-hundred-year-old headboard and he would rather have the place empty than rent to a group again.

Charles offered to go out to the island and try to find another place. No chance. All seven of us wanted to go with him. For two hundred and seventy-three dollars you want to see what you're getting, right? So, on a cold Sunday in March (March is the hunting season), in layers and layers of sweaters, the eight of us shlepped out to the island on the ferry. It was cold, and Charles Miller and his roommate snuggled up. The Ponties were on opposite sides of the boat.

We had no need for the New York *Times*' classified or the local newspaper—something with columns like "Barefeet and Wagons"—for there are many, many rental agents on Fire Island ready to rent you the tiny little bungalows, promising furniture where there is none, raving about wood-burning fireplaces and mentioning words that would appeal to Manhattanites, like rustic and quaint. We wanted rustic and quaint!

We saw several cottages, all with names, Little Lila and Home and Nana's Nook. (Cherry Grove has better names. The one I like is Four Boys Only.) Can eight assorted strangers find a dream home? It's hard. Little Lila didn't have a refrigerator. We all agreed to nix that—me first. Sal's Sand Home had a fireplace, but it was in the bedroom. Could we make the bedroom the living room? No, it wouldn't work, and it just isn't fair that some people could toast their tootsies while others couldn't. Hilda's Hideaway was right opposite the movie, and since that was the only movie in town, it would be noisy when the feature broke. Mrs. Pontie thought of that. Mr. Pontie disagreed with her and made her cry.

We found a place. Papa's Getaway. A little more money than we wanted to pay—seventeen dollars more per person. A little less than gorgeous. Last summer's sand was still on the floor. A little less furnished than

106

we expected—three wrought-iron chairs with torn canvas covers and four double beds. But it was the best of the lot and, naturally, the rental agent told us another group was very interested and she already had their check, but that we seemed much more respectable. Two girls panting for men, two fags, a fighting husband and wife, a girl in a loud poncho who never talked and a guy who ground out cigarettes on the floor in every house we were in. We looked more respectable than what?

So we were rentees. Rentees, I might add, who missed the midafternoon ferry and had to wait in the nothingness for hours and hours until the next ferry left. I looked at the group and realized for the first time that I was going to sleep in a house with all these strangers. This wasn't my mother and father and my sister, Melissa. These people, except for Linda, were strangers. I found out later by talking to other rentees that there is always this moment when you realize these strangers are going to share your toilet seat.

There were two groups. Group A and Group B, named by yours truly—such imagination. The A group was Linda and me and Agatha Horowitz and Mark Marks. The two happy couples, the Ponties and the Charles Millers, were in Group B. Our group got to go out first, which on the surface looks like a big advantage, but take it from Sheila, it's not. If you ever have a choice, get in Group B. By the time Group B went out the place was in working order. They had a nice relaxing weekend, all cozy and comfy.

When you go out first, you get to clean up the place, and guess who never got to get on the beach because she was mopping? When you go out first, you freeze because you never bothered to find out that the place didn't have heat and you didn't know to bring your quilt and Doctor Dentons. When you go out first, you don't have any hot water because the gas heater

107

isn't hooked up and you're Jewish and so you don't know from heaters. You look high and low for a plumber and pay him a fortune when you go out first. And you wanna know the worst thing about going out first? You buy the staples—the salt and pepper and sugar and toilet paper, the basil and oregano and jam and butter.

I learned the first week that all food was ridiculously expensive on the island—like fifty cents for a tomato. I'm sure Happy Rockefeller wouldn't pay fifty cents for a tomato. What you had to do—if you wanted to eat, and you know that I did—was shop on the mainland and bring your groceries out with you on the ferry. It's not bad. There are a lot of tanned kids with sun-bleached hair waiting with their red wagons for the ferry to come in, in hopes of helping you to your house for a quarter. So I shlepped the groceries out and learned that no matter how much I loved chocolate chip mint ice cream, it wasn't gonna make it.

The first weekend was quiet. Linda sort of liked Mark Marks, Agatha kept to herself and I was too busy cleaning and buying to really have the same kind of luck that Linda's cousin Rhoda had, but I wasn't rushing things. It was too cold to go to the beach, which I was very happy about. It gave me an extra two weeks to look good in a bathing suit.

The second time Group A went out, I noticed we needed a set of house rules. Group B left the house a mess. Group B didn't turn off the water heater, and behind Group A's back, they had allowed strangers to use the house during the week. One of them stayed right on into Group A's weekend.

Posted by me on the kitchen door, everyone should see it:

1. RENTEES OF THIS HOUSE SHOULD BE CONSIDER-ATE OF OTHER RENTEES BY MAKING SURE THAT THE HOUSE IS CLEAN WHEN THEY LEAVE.

2. DID YOU REMEMBER TO TURN OFF THE WATER HEATER WHEN YOU LEFT? REMEMBER, GAS COSTS MONEY AND ALL RENTEES ARE RESPONSIBLE FOR THE GAS BILL.

3. DID YOU REMEMBER TO TURN OFF THE LIGHTS WHEN YOU LEFT? REMEMBER, ELECTRICITY COSTS MONEY AND ALL RENTEES ARE RESPONSIBLE FOR THE ELECTRIC BILLS.

4. WERE YOU CONSIDERATE OF OTHER PEOPLE'S BELONGINGS? PLEASE DO NOT TOAST OTHER PEOPLE'S MARSHMALLOWS.

5. IF YOU HAVE INVITED GUESTS TO STAY AT THE HOUSE, PLEASE INFORM THEM THAT THEY WILL BE CHARGED TWO DOLLARS A NIGHT. THIS WILL APPLY TO THE GAS AND ELECTRIC BILLS.

6. DON'T TRACK SAND.

7. ASK YOURSELF WHEN YOU LEAVE—HAVE I DONE EVERYTHING THAT I SHOULD HAVE THIS WEEKEND?

The list was taken down by some pervert, and a "Fuck you" was put in its place. I made several more lists, put them through the Xerox while Mrs. Cox wee-weed and kept posting them.

By Group A's fourth weekend, Linda and Mark Marks were in love, slipping off behind dunes—and Linda was tanned all over, so you figure it out. I got to know Agatha Horowitz a lot better, which was nice, but not worth two hundred and ninety bucks.

Agatha was a teacher, but not the regular kind. She was a speech specialist who traveled from school to school in her district, which was downtown Brooklyn. She got to call the kids out of the classrooms and teach them on a one-to-one relationship. This excited Agatha Horowitz.

"Would you like to go to the beach with me, Sheila?" (Agatha spoke softly and carried a big book. Everyone carries big books. I had *The Decline and*

Fall of the Roman Empire because I wanted to attract an intellectual.)

"Sure. Wait until I get into a suit." (Agatha gave me the confidence to get into a suit. She had a few lumps herself.)

We sat on the beach, looking and burning. Not realizing we were doing either one. I read the first paragraph of *The Decline and Fall of the Roman Empire* over and over again.

If you have nothing better to do than look on the beach, Fire Island is a nice place to look. Very white sand and very blue water. There are taxis that run along the beach and great-looking children running in packs. All the children had straight hair, which reconfirmed my desire not to marry Norman. He had wavy hair and I had wavy hair and our children would never come out looking like the ones I saw on the beach. Forget Norman. Never see him again. But wait! Don't throw out dirty water until you have clean. Forget Norman—but not yet.

Agatha and I did meet some people. The beach got more and more crowded, and our beach blanket eventually got surrounded by other beach blankets. More blankets made bridges, and the group got more and more intertwined. "Where are you from?" . . . "I live on East Sixty-seventh." . . . "What do you do?" . . . "Do you know Leslie Rutley, she's from Franklin Square." . . . "Where'd you go to school?" . . . "Do you know Harriet Busk? She went there." . . . "What street you on here?" . . . "That's right near us." . . . "Your first year out here?" . . . "Yeah, it's great." . . . "The city is impossible." . . . "Do you know?" . . . "Do you know?" . . . Lots of Jewish geography. We met a lot of nice people, but all at once. No one-to-one relationship here.

Those members of the group who had been there the year before talked about the year before. They all

110

felt that the year before was much better than this year. By this time last year, the third weekend into July, things were really happening. There was skinny dipping in the ocean. There were nude volleyball games. Nude swimming? Nude volleyball? I hardly took nude showers. If you want to know the truth, only the people with great figures were regretting the lack of tushy-showing.

Everyone missed the volleyball games (both dressed and undressed). Why? Because volleyball is a Jewish sport. It's fun, and nobody can get hurt.

So the people who were new to the island asked the people who were there last year why things were so good last year and so bad this year. There was a simple explanation. There were better people out last year. That made the new people feel great. There was silence for a minute, and then one girl rolled down the top of her bathing suit to the waist so she wouldn't get strap marks. That seemed to break the ice. We went back to asking "Do you know?" By the end of the day I still had no idea how the Roman Empire declined and fell. As we were packing up, the girl who had stripped to the waist (my eyes had avoided her all afternoon) invited us over for Sangria, sixish.

Agatha and I went back to Papa's Getaway and changed, trying to look casual, taking great care. Linda and Mark joined us. Linda was tanned. I was burned. She looked great in her faded jeans. My jeans never faded—they just grew too tight.

We went to two houses and dined on chips and avocado dips, and about ten of us ended up at Flynn's Hotel-Restaurant-Bar, having Cokes and beer and still trying to find out if we had any friends in common.

That was Fire Island. Days on the beach, houses at night. A lot of strange faces popping up all over the place, sometimes in your bed.

By the fifth weekend I spent out there, someone fell

111

in love with me. Thought I was beautiful, wanted a permanent relationship. You may even know the person . . . Agatha Horowitz.

"Mom, this is Agatha Horowitz. We're in love."

"Manny, how could that be? I've heard of two boys doing things. I hear it's quite common. But two girls?"

Just for the record, the idea of a lesbian relationship repulsed me. No tendencies, no desire. The last time I held hands with a girl was in fifth grade. I used to walk hand in hand with Ruthie, but all little girls do that, and Sheila Levine had outgrown it completely. So what do I do with Agatha was the question. You see, the problem was she started slowly before I knew what she was doing and what she was, and I was friendly. I must have said a thousand things to lead her on.

"Sheila?"

"Yes, Agatha?"

"What do you think of me?" (I thought she had an inferiority complex or something and needed some building up.)

"I think you're very nice." (Right thing to say, right? Right thing to say to anyone but a dyke.) Pop, tell Mom what a dyke is.

"Just nice?"

"Very nice. A nice girl, Agatha. I mean nice, friendly, sweet, clean." (I didn't know at this point what Agatha, the Sheila-lover, was getting at.)

"I think you're very nice, too."

Later that very same night, folks, we were getting dressed to go to one of those "sixish" things.

"Sheila?" (Was there a twinkle in her eye?)

"Yes, Agatha?"

"Do you really feel like going tonight? I thought maybe just the two of us could sit around and talk, and you know." (I didn't know.)

112

"I'd like to go. We could talk later."

"Okay. I'll go, too."

I had really wanted to go because I had heard that the party was at a good house. Like sororities and fraternities on campuses, there were good and bad houses on Fire Island. Also, an old philosophy of mine from way back was never give up a group. You never know when an Aquarius who was destined to marry you is going to show up in some group.

When we got there, Agatha wouldn't leave my side. Even if Mr. Right was there, he couldn't find room to get near me. Flynn's again and then home, Agatha still at my side. Closer than my side. Brushing up against me. I may be exaggerating now that I know what she was up to. I may be imagining things that weren't there, but so help me God, that girl was brushing.

When we got back to the cottage, I fluffed up the cushions, a onceover on the Formica (the vacuum cleaner didn't work. There wasn't a vacuum cleaner on the island that worked), and started to undress. I was being watched.

"Sheila?"

"Yes, Agatha?"

"You said we could talk later."

"One minute, just let me get comfortable. We'll talk if you want to."

I got into my stunning flannel nightgown, all red and white and nylon lace with bows. Warm and functional. (Like me.)

"What do you want to talk about, Agatha?"

"Sheila?"

"Yes, Agatha?" (All our conversations seemed to begin this way.)

"I don't know if you've noticed it or not, but I've been pretty depressed lately." (I hardly knew her, so

113

I hadn't really noticed, but when someone tells you they're depressed and they've been brushing up against you, you're going to take their word for it, right?)

"What's the matter?" (I'm thinking, she's got problems? She should know the problem I have. Maybe if I told her my problem, her problems would seem minor. And why limit myself to Agatha? If I told thousands of girls my problems, thousands of girls would be uplifted. Is there a foundation set up for problem telling? Would they give me a grant? I would tour the country—a one-woman show. The lights go out; the audience gets quiet; I appear in a simple blue suit. I clear my throat. I begin, "So, you think you have problems . . . ?")

"Sheila?"

"Yes, Agatha?"

"I had this very close relationship, and it's over, and I never wanted it to be over." She cried into her pillow.

"How do you know it's over? Maybe it's just a lover's quarrel. You'll apologize, and everything will be all right."

"No. It's over." (Sob . . . sob . . . sob)

"So you'll find someone else."

"I have found someone else, but that person doesn't seem to like me."

"How do you know, Agatha?"

"The person just doesn't seem to want to be with me as much as I want to be with them." (Sob . . . sob . . . sob)

"But you're just guessing at this, Agatha. Maybe the other person likes you just as much as you like him; only he's shy about it, too. Why don't you stop playing games and tell the other person how you feel about him?"

"It's hard."

"I know it's hard, but do it, Agatha. That's the only way you'll find out."

114

"Sheila, I love you."

"Thank you, Agatha. I'm sure if you follow my advice, things will work out."

"Sheila, you don't understand. It's you I love. You're the person I want to be with. Do you feel anything for me?" (Oh, boy!)

Pretty good. Only my fifth weekend and I had already gotten a proposal. Yeckh! How do girls do it with other girls? I mean I know *how* they do it. I don't know how they *do* it.

And I learned something—pay attention and write this down—Mother, you listen too, you never know when the lady in the bakery who throws an extra cookie in your bag is going to make a pass. My observation is:

FACT: IT IS NOT EASY TO SHAKE A LESBO.

I had to change from Group A to Group B. Linda and I traded with the Ponties. Linda didn't care because she hated Mark Marks from the moment that she found out his parents had voted for Nixon. Miss Minsk was getting harder and harder to please. I had to change my telephone number. Three times a day Agatha Horowitz called me to find out what was wrong with her, just because I didn't particularly care to touch her nipples. Eventually I had to get an unlisted number, which didn't suit Linda, so she got her own phone. Two phones in a one-room apartment with alcoves.

I almost had to move. There were many mornings, when I looked out the window, I would see dirty taxis, dirty buses, dirty people and dirty-minded Agatha Horowitz. She stood across the street and stared up at my window. I bought lined drapes.

Just like I tried to "accidentally" bump into Ivan the beautiful, Agatha tried to bump into me. I'd be coming out of 1650 Broadway, the end of a day spent Xeroxing squirrel music, and there would be Agatha in the street outside the building.

"Oh, hi, Sheila, I was just on my way to a friend who lives down the block."

"Great, Agatha, I'm on my way to see a friend myself." (I could see the hurt where the twinkle used to be. It's not easy being a love object.)

"Wanna have coffee or something?" (I'd have coffee, but I wanted nothing to do with the "or something.")

"I'd like to, Agatha, but really, I'm late. This friend and I are going to an early movie, and we have to be there at six thirty-two. [I looked at my watch and registered horror on my face.] Oh, my God, I'm late. Nice seeing you, Agatha." (And off I ran into the pointed end of somebody's umbrella. Let me ask you this: How come Doris Day with all her good looks never ran into an Agatha Horowitz?)

There were phone calls. (She always managed to find my unlisted number.)

"Sheila?"

"Yes, Agatha?"

"Why don't you like me?"

"Agatha, I do like you. Really, you're a very nice person. I just don't want to . . . you know . . . have that kind of . . . you know . . . that kind of relationship."

"How do you know?"

"I don't know. I mean, I'm not putting it down. I'm sure it's great for some people. It must be really fantastic when you dig that sort of thing. But honest to God, Agatha, I never have and I never will dig that sort of thing."

"How do you know if you've never tried it? I thought the same way that you did a couple of years ago. I even used to date boys. Then I met this girl, Maxine, and she was very gentle and we were friends at first and then the relationship grew and pretty soon, Sheila, I wanted to make love to her and we did it and it was fantastic."

116

Two hundred and ninety dollars, not including the fortune I spent on staples, and I end up with Agatha Horowitz on my line every night. I'll say one thing— she promised to call me in the city and she did.

Group B had Labor Day. Labor Day weekend is always frantic. It's the last chance before the summer is over. If you don't meet someone by Labor Day weekend, it means you've spent the summer without a summer romance.

No one slept. (People fuck, but they don't sleep.) Everyone was on the beach from early morning trying to get deeper tans so that they will last into the winter. There was a mass exchange of addresses and telephone numbers. Before this weekend, we expected to see people back on the island. Now you knew they could be lost in Manhattan, the Bronx and Staten Island, too, unless you recorded them in your little leather address book with the blue pages and the gold edges. One frantic girl tried to sign people up for a house on the island for the following year. She had no luck. Not one person was willing to admit they were coming back.

And there were parties. Last parties, people frantically trying to stretch their weekend. We were invited "sixish, sevenish," which went on to "threeish, fourish." People just didn't want to let go of the summer.

On Labor Day we had the responsibility of closing up Papa's Getaway. (The disadvantage of being in Group B.) We turned off the lights, cleaned up the place and had the water heater disconnected.

Thirty-nine people took the last ferry back, straw satchels beside them, sheets and pillows in their arms. We'll do it again next year.

The Wedding (Not Mine)

W E DID GO BACK to Fire Island the following summer . . . and the following summer. Then we were the ones who were saying, "The island was much more fun last year." We didn't go back for a fourth year. We had graduated. Fire Island was for kids . . . "Did you notice that the crowd on the island is getting younger and younger every year?" . . . "The place is full of high school kids. . . . And it's so noisy there." . . . "Who wants strange people in your house night and day?" . . . "And it has gotten so dirty." . . . We were aging. We went the way of other New Yorkers of our age and background. We went to East Hampton.

The Hamptons—a little more expensive, a little older crowd. You needed a car, or there was no way to get around. Linda went out and found a great house and put together an interesting group. I just went. Spent every weekend in East Hampton for the entire summer and didn't put on a bathing suit once. People were now wearing bikinis. Little teeny, tiny bikinis dotting the beaches.

It was a nice, relaxing summer, a few brunches and a few dinners. Norman came out a couple of times and looked ridiculous in the jeans I bought him so that he would look like everyone else. (He would never look like everyone else. He had no desire to grow long sideburns or a mustache or anything.) I found out after the summer was over that the people in our very house

118

were having group sex. That was no fair, kids. I chipped in, too.

On Fire Island there are no phones, which is a blessing when you have a mother like mine.

"No phones? Sheila, darling, what happens, God forbid, I have to get in touch with you?" She said that at least once a week.

There are phones in the Hamptons, which relieved my mother tremendously. This way, she could call me on weekends to remind me that I was single. I made her swear to God that she wouldn't call me unless it was an emergency.

"Suppose I have to tell you we won't be home all day."

"Mother, that is not an emergency."

"Suppose I don't feel well."

"That is not an emergency."

"What is an emergency with you?"

"Death. That is an emergency."

One Sunday night, just as I was taking my famous quiche out of the oven, she called.

"Sheila, dear?"

"Yes, Mom?" (I was really upset. I had said, "death.")

"I have some news." (The way she said it, I thought there had been a mass murder on the block and she was the prime suspect.)

"Yeah?"

"Your sister is engaged. She's getting married next October."

Worse. It was worse than mass murder. How can she get married before I do? How could Luci Baines do it to Lynda Bird? I won't go. I'll hide. I'll go to California and hide, and no one will know where to find me. I don't wish her well. I hope something terrible happens and she can't get married. I'll tell her future husband that there is a history of craziness in our family, and because of certain things Melissa has done, we're sure she inherited it.

Mom, how could you? Don't let this happen to me. Don't make me go to the wedding with all those people asking me when my turn is. I don't know when my turn is. I don't have a turn! Mama, don't let her get married first. Stop her. Please!

Once I got over the initial hysteria, I was able to think clearly. I came to this conclusion. Melissa is thin. Melissa is getting married. Therefore, thin people get married. Those were my first thoughts. On the Long Island Railroad the wheels seemed to be saying, "Sheila, lose some weight. . . . Sheila, lose some weight. . . . Sheila, lose some weight." Joan of Arc's voices came to me. They told me I could lose a good twenty pounds. It was all so simple. Even if I didn't get married the minute I was thin, at least I could be thin at the wedding. Thin people look as if they have a choice.

"Mom, I'm going on this diet. . . ."

"Are you sure you eat enough?"

"Yes, Mother, I'm sure I eat enough. I'm sure I eat more than enough. In my life I've eaten enough for the whole city of Trenton, New Jersey, Mother. If you lined all the Chinamen in the world four abreast, they wouldn't have eaten as much as I did at the hors d'oeuvres table at the last Bar Mitzvah I attended. If I stopped eating for one day . . . for one day only . . . you could feed all the starving people in India. And you ask if I eat enough? Why do you ask now, Mother? Why didn't you ask when I was a baby and you kept shoving it in? When I was a baby, you cried when I didn't eat. You've told me many times that my little legs were so skinny you cried at the doctor's office. There was nothing to my behind, you said. Well, take a look! There's a lot there now, Mother!

Not only did you cry when I didn't eat—you put on a circus so I would eat. As you shoveled your spoonfuls, you had a little game. Here's one for Mommy and one for Daddy and one for Grandma Arnold and one for Grandpa Arnold and one for Nana and one for Aunt Phyllis and one for Uncle Larry and on and on until your adult appetite was satisfied. And when I made all gone, there was rejoicing. There was rejoicing in the streets. Clap hands. Clap hands. Sheila finished.

When I was very little, the war was on my head. There were children starving in Europe, so I had to eat. As I grew up, you comforted me with food.

"Here, precious darling, don't worry that you can't put the bead on the string. Have a cookie."

You know what's really cute, Mother? How your attitude changed. Boom! Just like that, your attitude changed when my sister, Melissa, was born. You said, "I had such a hard time with Sheila, this one I'm leaving alone. If she wants to eat, fine. If she doesn't want to eat, fine. I'm tired of aggravating myself." You didn't play fair. Why didn't you stuff Melissa, too? Why didn't you let me not eat? Fine. You know what they say about your darling Sheila? . . . "She has such a pretty face. If only she'd lose fifteen pounds, she'd be a real beauty." . . . Shit! I'm a member of the Diet Pepsi Generation. In my lifetime I've lost those fifteen pounds at least seven times. That's more than a hundred pounds. But it keeps coming back. It keeps coming back because I expect someone to clap hands every time I eat.

Being overweight is one of the reasons I'm going to kill myself. I'm tired of dieting, and I'm tired of looking at everyone else in bikinis. I'd stick a knife in my chest, but it would probably never get through the fatty tissue to my heart.

I heard of this Doctor (I capitalize doctor because to a Jewish girl, a doctor is a Doctor) called Dr. Sheldon, who gave loads and loads of diet pills to girls

121

like me, willing to spend ten dollars for the first session, five dollars thereafter, for those little rainbow pills in the white cardboard box.

The wedding was only thirteen months off. I called the good doctor and made the earliest available appointment, Tuesday at twelve. Therefore, Monday night was a Farewell to Food Night for me. That's when I eat everything I can get my hands on because I know I'm going on a diet the next day. There have been many of them. I ate potato salad and potato knishes. I ate corned beef and cream cheese on rye. I ate chopped liver and rocky road ice cream. And I ate an entire container of Cool Whip.

"I don't understand it, nurse. I mean, I have no idea why all of a sudden I put on fifteen pounds. There must be something wrong with my glands, or it's inherited or something. I don't eat that much."

"Mrs. Levine [I hated her], would you mind taking your shoes off and stepping on the scale so that we can get your correct weight?" Step on the scale? Right here in the middle of the afternoon with my clothes on? You can't do that to me. I'm an American. I have my rights! I stepped on the scale but didn't look. I could feel her hand move one of those little weights from the hundred slot to the hundred and fifty slot. I was over one fifty. Oh, God. If only I hadn't had the Cool Whip.

"One fifty-seven. Thank you." (Thank you for what? Thank you for being a hundred and fifty-seven pounds and dragging myself to Dr. Sheldon?)

She took some medical history and my blood pressure and asked me without blinking an eye if there was obesity in my family. I was not obese. I had a little baby fat . . . prepregnancy fat?

I was sent into a small meeting room with a lot of folding chairs facing front. Already seated there (some needed two chairs) were a lot of chubby people. I was the smallest of the group. What an uplift! It's like all of a sudden you're the skinny sister. One really Cool-Whipped woman wanted to know what I was doing there with a figure like mine.

We had a lecture about fish and chicken without skin and don't eat anything that's not on the list (there were like three things on the list) and raise your hand if you retain water. Our lecturer was a woman of sixty-seven with an Annette Funicello body. Boy, was I gonna listen to her. We each got a box of purple, brown, pink and green pills. Take them all and don't forget your vitamins. Just to make sure, we all swallowed our pink pill together before we left the room.

Guess what? I have a tendency to retain water. I needed that, right? When I went back a week later to get weighed, I wore lighter clothes, no jewelry and had had my hair cut an inch. I had taken every pill faithfully and lost three pounds. Not enough for Dr. Sheldon, and by the way, where the hell was the great Dr. Sheldon? I had been to the office twice and had not seen him once. Maybe Dr. Sheldon was overweight and afraid to show his big ass.

The lady rearranged my pills—gave me some more because I retain water. Sure I retain water. I retain everything else. So I took the new little yellow pills and peed a lot. Couldn't wait to go back.

Let me tell you a little something about diet pills. They're psychologically disturbing. If you're anything like me, you take a diet pill and you defy them all day. You keep saying to yourself—okay, diet pill, you're not going to change my life and my eating habits. I'm going to prove to Dr. Sheldon and all the people who manufacture the pills that they don't work. I'm gonna take them and I'm gonna eat. Period.

They did work—made me crazy, head-scratching, nail-biting crazy. I was on the ceiling, shouting at Mrs. Cox, kicking mailboys and slamming the door on the doorman's fingers on purpose.

"Sheil, I hate to pry, but is something bothering you?"

"NO, LINDA, WHY DO YOU ASK? WHY DO YOU ALWAYS ASK STUPID QUESTIONS? YOU'RE ALWAYS PRYING AND ASKING. NOW LEAVE ME ALONE. JUST GO AWAY AND LEAVE ME ALONE."

"Sheila, you want me to come over tonight?"

"SHUT UP, NORMAN. SHUT UP AND LEAVE ME ALONE."

"Sheila, darling, it's Mother. How are you?"

"OH, MOTHER, WHY DO YOU KEEP ASKING PERSONAL QUESTIONS?"

By the fourth visit I had lost thirteen pounds and five friends.

I had my hair straightened and frosted; the ends broke, but what the hell, I liked it. I had my nails polished and bought false lashes that I wore but never quite got to stick. And then what?

What's one of the first things you do when you lose thirteen pounds? Saturday shopping. A ritual in New York. The girls of New York know where to shop and just where to find things. Linda knew, at least, and she showed me the way.

Ohrbach's for pocketbooks and fur-lined gloves, boots on the second floor if you couldn't afford the ones in Lord & Taylor, which were more expensive but they looked it. You gets what you pays for. And Ohrbach's for stockings. Saks for belts and things and Saks for sales. And Saks for wrinkle cream. Yeah, I was in the market for moisturizers now. Altman's— not really, an occasional tailored something. Up the street to Bonwit's and then Bloomingdale's. God bless Bloomingdale's, where you can always find it even if you can't find it anywhere else. From the bargain basement to the boutiques, we examined everything—on every rack. I had four or five soft pretzels on the way. Gained back two pounds.

Linda found everything she needed . . . and on sale yet. I had to search and search, for simple things like black slacks. Linda bought accessories that hit her fancy. I bought only what I needed—in practical colors. A hat that doesn't show the snow, a sweater that I don't exactly love but is washable. As a result of shopping habits, Linda looked like she walked out of a boutique and I looked like I'd wash well.

We shlepped the packages back home, walking all the way, and I thought:

"Oh, God, I shouldn't have spent all that money. . . . So what, you charged it. You won't even see the bills for another month. . . . Yeah, but I really shouldn't charge. . . . It's silly. . . . You get the bills eventually and then you're miserable when you get them. . . . So, I'll pay them off little by little. . . . No, I can't do that. . . . That's being in debt. . . . I'll never, never be in debt! . . . Maybe I should close down all the charge accounts and only pay cash for things? . . . Why do I worry? Linda doesn't worry that she just bought herself a twenty-dollar Gucci wallet. . . . Why do I worry about a few bills? I'm working. . . . Suppose I lose my job and can't afford the apartment and starve to death? . . . These pants are great. . . . Maybe I should go to Bloomingdale's on Thursday night and pick up a top to go with them. . . . I'll charge it."

Well, I didn't keep the weight off. Two weeks later the only thing that still fit from that shopping trip was the hat. If they can send men to the moon, why can't they cure the fat right here in our own backyard?

In April, just six months before the wedding, Linda moved out to live with a fifty-year-old French furrier (just like in the movies) and Joshua moved in. I hadn't seen Joshua in almost a year since he had "married" this guy. One night he just showed up, instinctively knowing there was room in the apartment. I welcomed him with open arms and started buying whole chickens instead of chicken parts.

Poor Joshua. He happened to land back on the convertible sofa just as I was getting really desperate. He saw me as a friendly sister, a girl friend, an aunt and mother. How sweet. I saw him as a front.

It's funny how I preferred Joshua to Norman. If you rated them both on a scale from one to ten, they'd both come up with about a four and a half. Norman was boring in bed. Joshua never slept with me, even if we shared a room. Norman had a boring job that paid little. If I married him, I could never buy my kids clothes in Saks. Joshua had no job. He always had about two dollars in his pocket that he got from I know not where. He had no job, but he might be a star someday, and I could charge up a storm. Norman had no looks. Joshua was very good-looking, but he spent hours in front of the mirror confirming those good looks.

Norman lived isolated from people. Joshua lived off people. Joshua doesn't ask questions. Norman asks the wrong ones. Norman laughed at dirty jokes. Joshua laughed at Lenny Bruce. Norman used ball-point pens, Joshua fountain pens. Norman is, therefore, vinyl. Joshua is genuine leather. And Norman was heterosexual, Joshua homosexual. Yeah, about four and a half points apiece. But Joshua wasn't boring.

Remember when Linda liked Charles Miller? Remember when I discussed girls who marry gay guys just because they wanted to be married? I, Sheila Levine, was willing to walk down the aisle with Joshua even though I knew the groom was prettier than the bride AND even though the groom would not be interested in sleeping with the bride. Yeah, I would have done it.

"Joshua?"

"Yeah?"

"I wonder what the people in the neighborhood are thinking about you and me—you living here and all."

"I don't think the people in the neighborhood really think about it."

"But if they were thinking about it, what would they be thinking?"

"I don't know."

"I think they'd be thinking that we're making it."

"So they're thinking that we're making it. Does that bother you?"

"No. It doesn't bother me at all. I wouldn't even care if they thought we were in love or engaged or something."

"Sheila, don't worry about it. They've got other things to think about."

"And what do you think about us?"

"Whadda you mean?"

"Isn't it funny, just the two of us—here alone all the time . . . some of the time? It's like we're engaged or married or something."

"Do you want me to move out? I'll move out anytime you want me to. I can move in with this guy."

"No, no. I like having you here, Joshua. Did you ever think of having kids—like having a wife so that you could have kids or something?"

"Sure. I've thought about it. Someday I guess I'd like to have kids."

"Did you ever think of getting married? Like to someone who really understood you and everything and let you sort of alone?"

"Whadda you mean?"

"Someone who liked you and whom you liked, and the two of you understood each other and everything."

"They don't work out."

"Whadda *you* mean?"

"Marriages like that don't work out. The wife gets upset that the kids don't have a he-man to look up to. Sheila, I sleep with guys. You don't want me."

"I want you, Joshua. I don't care that you sleep with guys. You could still sleep with guys. I swear to God, you could sleep with guys any night of the week and I wouldn't care. We could have kids."

"Sheila, you're a middle-class girl. You need a nice Jewish boy. Come on, Sheila. You don't want me."

"I do."

And he moved out. One day I came home and Joshua wasn't there. A lot of days when I came home he wasn't there, but this time he really wasn't there. His things were gone. Empty.

Dear Sheila,
  I'm saving you from me. Someday when you're married with three little girls running after you, I'll come visit. You'll be living with a man who makes love to you and maybe an occasional other woman, and I'll be happy for you.

                              Love,
                              JOSHUA
                              (alias Alan Goldstein)

Linda moved back. She found out that the French furrier, Bernard Le Berjeau, was really Bernie Goldblum from the Bronx. His wife called one day when he was out and told her.

"And, Sheil, I wasn't so upset that he changed his name and tried to make a new life for himself. But when I found out that he had no opinion on the Israeli-Arab conflict, it turned my stomach. I wouldn't care if he was pro-Arab, but no opinion—it turned my stomach."

My mother was really very sorry. She hadn't planned for Melissa to get married first. It just happened that
128

way. She said she was sorry many times, and each time she said it, I bit her head off. "WHAT ARE YOU SO SORRY ABOUT? IF I WANTED TO BE MARRIED, I WOULD BE MARRIED. NOW GET OFF MY BACK."

Analysis. Surprisingly enough, Melissa's wedding and my seeking professional help for my troubled mind came at about the same time.

I knew I needed help. Every time I thought of Melissa's wedding, I wheezed, coughed, got a facial tic, and fell down on the street. I had a hint that something was bothering me.

Joshua once told me about the William Alanson White Clinic, 20 West Seventy-fourth. I tried, but there was a waiting list, and I was twitching. When you twitch, you don't wait six months.

Believe me, I couldn't afford it. But I also couldn't afford to get a facial tic at this point in my life. Okay, so I went . . . to three different doctors. I really couldn't communicate with any of them.

Doctor number one—he shall remain anonymous, not because I choose not to name him, but because he's a lousy psychiatrist. He was semi-Freudian. Believed in Freud, but he talked to me. For thirty dollars an hour, I at least wanted questions.

"And, Doctor, if you really want to know the truth [no, he wanted lies], what really bothers me is my sister's wedding. Isn't that silly? Ha. Ha. Ha. Isn't it silly . . . a grown-up, single girl like me, who has no prospect of getting married in the near future . . . isn't it silly—ridiculous when you think about it—that I should get so upset over my sister's wedding? Isn't it silly? I mean, it's just a wedding. I'm not jealous or anything. I don't understand why I should be so upset. Do you?"

"Sheila, you've been coming to me about a month now. My guess is, Sheila, that you are running away from marriage."

129

What a shmuck! Do I sound to you like a girl who is running away from marriage? For Christ's sake, I proposed to Joshua—and Dr. Shmuck is guessing I'm running away from marriage.

Dr. Fink. Go ahead, laugh at the name. He's making a fortune and living on Park Avenue, and you're laughing.

"What do you want to be when you grow up, little boy Fink?"

"I want to be a big psychiatrist and live on Park Avenue and charge people thirty-five dollars an hour."

"And, Doctor, every time I think of my sister's wedding, I could throw up. I get this gagging sensation in my throat, and I don't know why. I'm very happy for my fucking sister, who's getting married before I am. I'm very happy for that fucking bitch."

Dr. Fink was also semi-Freudian. Had me lying down and talking about dreams a lot.

Came to this conclusion—are you ready for this? I'm going to tell you in one sentence what it cost me four hundred and ninety dollars to find out—I don't like myself, so how can I expect other people to like me. Yeah. Big help, Dr. Fink was. Not only did he tell me that, but he told me that he had a new partner and the new partner and he were going to share patients and he thought I'd do nicely with the new doctor —young Dr. Hirshfield.

"Dr. Hirshfield, my real problem is that I feel rejected. I thought Dr. Fink liked me and then he said I was going to be your patient and I really feel kinda rejected."

It cost me about three hundred dollars to get over my rejection from Dr. Fink. And Dr. Hirshfield didn't help. He was young and sort of pretty, in a psychiatrist sort of way. I mean, if I were doing a movie about Natalie Wood falling in love with her psychiatrist, I would look for a Dr. Hirshfield type. The real problem with Dr. Hirshfield was that he wore this tremendous wedding band. I couldn't keep my eyes off his wedding band.

Maybe someday they'll set up a Sheila Levine Memorial Fund, dedicated to the single girl and what makes her tick. Dr. Hirshfield, I would like to appoint you head doctor of that study. Use the money as you like. Do whatever you want. You have carte blanche. Only, please, take off the wedding band.

Melissa was marrying a Jewish "catch." Very nice boy, very nice parents, very nice penis. Mrs. Richard Hinkle. That's who my sister was going to be. He would have nothing to do with babies' hats, was going into real estate. Very nice. His parents lived in Lawrence, Long Island. Very nice. His parents gave the couple a thousand dollars as an engagement present. Very nice. Sheila was going to be maid of honor. Very nice? No, not very nice. I hadn't really ever been close to my sister, never liked her. Why do Jewish mothers force their siblings upon each other? I can hear her say it—"Melissa, I know Sheila would be very hurt if she wasn't maid of honor."

I wouldn't be hurt, really . . . don't even invite me to the wedding. . . . I would be delighted. . . . I may not be in town anyway. . . . I'm sure Melissa wouldn't mind at all. . . . I hardly know her. . . . She's a semi-acquaintance. I don't want to buy her a gift.

"Stop talking foolish, Sheila. Of course you're invited to the wedding. You're her sister." Then how come I'm fat and she's thin? How come my sweet sixteen was all girls because I didn't have a boyfriend? How come Melissa's sweet sixteen was co-ed in the basement with the boys putting their hands down the girls' scoop-neck dresses?

Mother cared. Bought me a dress, twice as expensive as Melissa's. Blue chiffon—to match the blue tablecloths and centerpieces and the blue bridesmaids and the blue cigarettes and the blue matches—"Melissa and Richard."

Norman sat back and watched the pretty wedding being planned. Isn't it nice—Melissa getting married?

My mother and Norman talk. . . .

"Oy, am I busy. It's not easy planning a wedding, I'll tell you. This one has to be invited and that one has to be invited, I'm telling you . . . sigh . . . but I don't mind. I'm happy to do it for my Melissa, and I'll do the same for my Sheila when the day comes for her to be married." (Hint . . . hint . . . hint)

"That's nice. If there's anything I can do to help you, Mrs. Levine, just let me know." (Marry the big one, you shmuck. That would help.)

My father and Norman talk. . . .

"You know, Norman, I'm very happy that Melissa is getting married, and I'm very sad, too. It's not easy marrying off a daughter. You'll find that out when you have daughters of your own. I'm just glad that I'm going to be able to give Melissa and Richard a very nice gift of five thousand dollars *and* I'm *very* glad that I'll be able to give my daughter, Sheila, five thousand dollars too, maybe a little more." Wink. (Hint . . . hint . . . hint)

"That's very nice of you, Mr. Levine."

And since I was no longer in the mood to refuse his proposal, Norman and Sheila talk. . . .

"So what do you think of Melissa and Richard getting married? I think it's great. I mean, he's not my type, but he's her type, and they seem to be very happy. And they're making my parents very happy. I guess some day soon, I'm gonna have to take the step and get married myself, even though I've been holding out all these years." (Hint)

"I guess so."

My mother and I talk. . . . (Wrong. My mother talks, and I listen.)

"Has Norman ever mentioned marriage to you? It seems that you have been seeing him an awfully long time. You know each other so well and all. I was just wondering if he ever mentioned marriage or anything. It seems he should at least mention marriage or stop wasting your time."

"LEAVE ME ALONE! JUST LEAVE ME ALONE. HE ASKED ME A MILLION TIMES TO GET MARRIED. I DON'T WANT TO GET MARRIED AND GET TIED DOWN LIKE MELISSA, WHO'S A DYKE ANYWAY. JUST LEAVE ME ALONE!"

"Stop yelling and what's a dyke?"

Sheila and her psychiatrist talk. . . .

"Doctor, I don't know what's wrong with me. I like my sister, and I'm very happy for her. Really! But I'm having these dreams where I kill her by tying her to a tree and setting her on fire. I see the fire killing her, and I just stand there and laugh. What do you think these dreams mean?"

"What do you think they mean, Sheila?"

"I don't know. I have no idea. I love my shitty sister."

Do you know that I actually prayed that something terrible would happen and that there would be no wedding? My prayer was a simple one— Please, dear God, don't let Melissa get married.

My prayers were going unanswered. The invitations went out, her pattern was registered, and the gifts poured in. Three hundred people said, "Yes, we'd love to come and see Melissa get married and sit in the hot temple and eat the cold roast beef."

Please, dear God, don't let Melissa get married.

I went back to Dr. Sheldon's for more pills. I felt at least I had to look thin at the wedding.

"Oh, Mrs. Levine, we were expecting you back. I didn't think you were the type to keep it off. Step on

133

the scale, please. . . . Oh! Mrs. Levine, we have gained, haven't we?"

One week before the wedding. Dresses were getting altered. Pictures of the bride for the paper. I was praying a lot. Please, dear God. . . . And something terrible happened. Richard Hinkle's uncle died suddenly. Had a stroke and died. A blessing in disguise, they were saying. Did he die because of me? I asked God to stop the wedding. I didn't pray for this. Guilt.

"It's not nice to have a big wedding when Mr. Hinkle's only brother died. It's just not nice." . . . "He would have wanted you to go on with the wedding." . . . "It's just not nice."

Oh, God. It's not my fault. My analyst said it wasn't my fault.

"Call all the people. Tell them the wedding has been canceled." . . . "Uncle Herman would have wanted you to have it."

"Look, we'll have a small wedding in the rabbi's study. We'll cut down the list—only invite the immediate family and close friends. You know we have some friends who are closer than the family." And the Hinkles only invited the immediate family and close friends. But it was hard to leave people out.

You have never in your life seen anything like it. Picture this if you can. Fifty-three people in the rabbi's study, which is a small office—maybe twelve by twelve. Picture it. The flowers weren't canceled, so they lined the walls of the rabbi's study. Lining the halls to the rabbi's study were another fifty people. That's what happens when you tell two Jewish women to invite only close relatives and friends. People were everywhere. They could have had the fucking wedding in the temple. Fifty-three perspiring people were standing in that rabbi's study. I'll never know how they squeezed in.

Everyone was crabby, including Melissa, who made

a face when the rabbi said she could kiss the groom. The groom stepped on my foot instead of the wineglass. It was over very quickly. Thank you for coming and out. The happy couple, who spent one night at the airport hotel and left for Puerto Rico and the Virgin Islands, will be living in Queens.

"Thank you for coming." . . . "Sheila, dear, you look wonderful. When are you going to get married?" (Fuck off!) "Thank you for coming." . . . "Sheila, I didn't recognize you. You look wonderful. Pretty enough to be a bride yourself." . . . "Thank you for coming." . . . "Ted, look who's here. Sheila's here. Congratulations, Sheila. We can't wait to dance at *your* wedding."

I don't know how I lived through it. I don't know how. Norman by my side yet. I didn't go back to Manhattan after the wedding. I went to my old house, into my old room, and cried . . . that's all . . . just cried.

Enough Already

YOU'RE not going to believe it. . . . The phone rings.

"Hello."

"Hello, Sheila? [The voice sounds familiar but I have no idea who it is.] Sheila, it's Agatha Horowitz." (So now I know.)

"How are you, Agatha?"

"Fine, Sheila, I think about you all the time."

"That's nice." (What else can one say?)

"I was wondering if you changed your mind about me and everything."

"Well, to tell you the truth, Agatha, I haven't changed my mind. You're a very nice girl, Agatha, but I really don't feel that way . . . you know."

"Then you probably won't be hearing from me again. I won't bother you anymore."

"It's not that you're a bother, Agatha."

"Sheila, since you will have nothing to do with me, I'm getting married to this guy, Gary." (She's getting married? *She's* getting married?)

"That's very nice, Agatha. Congratulations." (I'm dying. Look, why don't you give this guy, Gary, to me and you find some girl who will appreciate you for what you really are, Agatha?)

"If you change your mind, Sheila. . . ."

She's getting married. Agatha Horowitz is registered at Tiffany's.

About a month after the phone call, I received a package—a beautiful gold bracelet from Cartier. The card—"I guess I'll always love you . . . Agatha"—engraved yet, "from A.H. to S.L. Always." So what could I do? "Thank you, Agatha, for the lovely bracelet, but I still haven't changed my mind. I have no desire to touch you in places that I already own. Sincerely, Sheila Levine." I sent the bracelet back once. It came back again. I wore it, but it always itched me.

Do you know what it's like? Do you have any idea what it's like to be a twenty-seven-year-old girl—woman—young lady, desperately looking for a husband in New York? You don't know unless you've lived it. You can't really know the hurt and the despair, the disappointment and the fear. Asking "When?" . . . "Is this my life?"

And I hated it. I was doing what all the single girls were doing—making appointments. If I didn't have a date with Norman, I was panicked. Absolutely had to find a way to spend the evening. The calls go from girl to girl on the company phones . . . "Hi, what're you doing tonight?" . . . "Want to meet for dinner and see a movie?" . . . "Want to see a show?" . . . "Why don't you come over?" . . . God forbid I had to go home alone. God forbid any of them went home alone.

These are the last-minute appointments. The appointments that say "Be with me tonight. I don't want to be alone." Oh, God, how many of those have I lived through? Worse than that, how many times was an appointment at the last minute broken because my friend got a date with a boy? . . . "I'm sorry, Sheila, can't make it tonight. This guy asked me out." Not that she liked the guy. Most of the time, she didn't, whoever it was. Any guy is better than going out with a girl. And no regard for the other party. An unwritten understanding. . . . We'll get together tonight if nothing better comes up.

137

And those awful nights when I came home alone with goodies from Horn & Hardart's Retail Shop, completely depressed. I'd end up eating and on the phone, calling everyone. Calling anyone.

The Sundays, when you do all those cultural things in the snow while the married people stay home in bed. All those cultural things that improve your mind, spoiling you so that you'll never be able to marry a non-New Yorker.

I met this guy once from Cleveland. He didn't know what restaurants to go to. He didn't know what was playing on Broadway. He just wasn't right for a sophisticated broad like me.

Some nights it was my turn to say, "I'm sorry," to a girlfriend because this guy asked me out—just a guy, nothing much. None of them took me fantastic places or bought me fantastic presents. (Agatha Horowitz's was the best present I ever got.) They didn't stimulate me, in or out of bed. I had one blind date after another. None of them were any better than Norman. I was drowning in dirty water.

And you do the Political Things. Knock on people's doors, urging them to vote. Licking envelopes at Democratic headquarters at night because your tongue isn't doing anything else. Sure, it's a good cause, but you're doing it because you have nothing else to do.

Then there were the nights Norman came over. They didn't change. So boring. Boring Norman with the boring sex. Sex with flecks.

We talked about marriage. No. Like my mother talking with her friend (the mother of the little boy), I was talking about marriage.

"Norman, this is silly. Really, it's just silly. You're here four nights a week. We're practically married now. Why don't we just sort of do it?"

"Do what?"

138

"Get married—you know." (There I go, proposing again.)

"Not now." (Not now? Not now, you say? Why not now? You leading a wild bachelor life out there in Brooklyn?)

"I just think it's silly, that's all. I mean, you pay for an apartment, and I pay for an apartment. And two can live as cheaply as one, ha . . . ha . . . ha. . . ."

"Nah."

Things did change that year. Linda drifted out of my life, went to Los Angeles on a vacation, got some sort of modeling job. Was living with a very important newspaperman. We kept in touch. There was an occasional long-distance telephone call, a hurried letter. . . . I'm fine. How are you? I thought I was in love with this guy, but it turns out he believes in capital punishment. . . . She breezed into New York once in a while and stayed with me, and we spent hours laughing about the good ol' days.

"And remember when we locked ourselves out?"

"And the Halloween party?"

"And the boys across the hall and Fire Island?"

"Oh, Linda, when did we get old?"

"We're not old. We're not even thirty."

"We're almost thirty. I'm using a moisturizer."

"Sheil, I'm using a moisturizer and Loving Care. Look." She bent her head down for me to look.

"I don't see any gray hair."

"That's because I use Loving Care."

"We are getting old, Linda."

"You're not kidding."

"How come we never got married?"

"I never met a guy who was normal. I'm not kidding. I could have gotten married a million times, only no one who ever was, you know, normal."

"I know what you mean. All the girls I know seem to be sane. The guys are all crazy."

139

"How many have you slept with?"

"I don't know. . . ."

"Guess."

"I don't know—ten . . . twenty."

"I've slept with thirteen guys—a baker's dozen. I can't believe it. You know, when we first moved to New York, I was a virgin."

"Me too." Almost.

"Thirteen guys and I've never had an orgasm. . . . Have you?"

"Yes, I think so."

"How do you know?"

"I don't know for sure. I said 'I think so.' "

"What's it like?"

"It's like . . . I don't know. I said I wasn't sure . . . a cold hot flash."

"I'm entitled to have an orgasm. It's my right. The first guy who gives me one, I'm going to marry."

"Even if he voted for Nixon?"

"If he voted for Nixon, he can't give orgasms. The first one who gives me an orgasm, I'm going to marry."

"Me too."

"I thought you had one."

"I said I wasn't sure."

Oh, Linda, what ever made us think it would all have a happy ending?

I changed jobs and moved. Yeah. I hired a van and moved to East Thirty-ninth, a doorman—safe but not chic. I was down to no roommates and no rooms. Just a small area for everything. I went into teaching, like Mama always wanted. It was like becoming a nun. I didn't make it in the real world, so I went into teaching. Thought about pensions and everything. I taught seventh-grade English on the Lower East Side. It wasn't easy; the kids were tough, but the job had its benefits. The pay was good—Christmas and Easter off, summer vacations. Yes, Mom, just like you said to me a long time ago.

I did everything I could to get married. I went to peace marches in the cold. . . . Maybe I'd meet a nice peacenik who wanted marriage. I went to rallies and night courses. I went back and forth to Dr. Sheldon. I went to every party I was invited to, every party I ever heard of. I went on a ski weekend and sprained my nose in the snow. I tried.

I got a Sassoon haircut, but it was too late. (Did you ever see an overweight girl with a really good haircut? It just doesn't look right.) And I worked for candidates and I subscribed to *Cosmopolitan*. Don't say I didn't try. I TRIED. The only thing I didn't do was move to Australia, where the men outnumber the women.

Do you have any idea how much money I have spent trying to get married? I estimate at least fifteen thousand dollars.

You figure—the beauty parlor and the clothes and the extra locks on the doors because you've living alone. It adds up. Then there's extra douching, good perfume and things like Pretty Feet. Late-night cab fares were a small fortune, not to mention certain psychiatrists. And theater tickets—I couldn't use twofers. I also know, in terms of dollars, why it's so nice to have a man around the house. It cost me six bucks to register for Computer Dating and four shleps called. And wrinkle creams and doormen and extra message units. And, Mr. President of these here United States, why isn't it tax-deductible? It was a loss.

One night I went out with Martha Katz—she's a friend from the school where I taught and was a frequent customer of Friday's, one of those singles' bars. Shortly after Friday's opened, Martha Katz went in. One night she took me. My mother taught me that bars

141

were for drunken goyim. Martha insisted that it was perfectly respectable for two young ladies, schoolmarms at that, to go into this house of alcoholic beverages.

So we went to Friday's on a Thursday night in pant suits—mine was a slenderizing black, rubbed away inside the thighs where the legs met.

The place was dark and phony. Nouveau culture. Who are they kidding with their low lights and their pretentious menu? Everything with wild rice. Half the people in the place would have preferred a corned beef on rye.

We ordered dinner, shishka-something, and tried to look very nonchalant, noticing everything that walked in and out of the door. Like Loeb Student Center, only now I was eating instead of reading. Everywhere around us unions were being made. Martha, a twenty-eight-year-old with adolescent skin, was getting rather anxious by dessert. It had taken us close to two hours to eat, and there wasn't much more we could do to extend the table time. The place was loaded with people, and the people were loaded in the place, but nothing much was happening for Sheila and Martha.

I must say the competition was stiff. Pretty young things with naturally straight hair squeezing through the crowd, bending over, giving us all a chance to look up their minis. Really beautiful girls. Like they were holding the Miss Universe contest there that night.

The guys were looking good, too. They were all the Arnolds and Harveys that I knew in high school; only they grew up and learned how to dress. Some fantastic in their pinstripe suits and the pinstripe shirts and the stripes on the ties. (And I bet you thought I was going to say and their pinstripe minds.) The ties. The ties you could die from—heavy, heavy silk, fifteen dollars a shot. I know. I once bought one for Norman in the hopes that he would look presentable at my sister's wedding. He forgot to wear it.

142

Some of the guys were casual—in the suede syndrome. Ever see a guy in the suede syndrome? You don't know what you're missing. Suede hats and jackets and suede pants. Nothing breathes, but they look great.

And an occasional guy trying to look as if he couldn't care less in a black turtleneck and jeans.

So just as we were finishing our apple cider, we were asked if we could be joined. Sure. A tall guy and a short guy, one in suede, one in pinstripe and, yes, Mother, one black and one white.

"Sheila, darling, I don't know why you're insinuating I don't like black people. A very nice black couple moved in down the block and she was over once."

Let's get everything straight. I am a liberal. I have frozen my tushy off in marches for my fellow black man. (Yes, I was looking while I was marching, but I *was* marching.) I have argued with my mother for hours and hours when she told me to be quiet in front of the maid. When I was asked to fill out a report at the school I taught on the color of my students, I couldn't think of what color the kids were. When I was in the "record business," I met, had coffee with many black kids. I sat and kibbitzed with black teachers at work and thought nothing of it. Okay, I'm great. Right? Wrong. The minute this black guy sat down at our table next to me, I felt funny, strange, choked up, didn't know what to say, was afraid that I would say the wrong thing, didn't open my mouth. I had never in my twenty-seven years been faced with a black person on a truly boy-to-girl level. AND I'M BEING HONEST. Give me credit for that, all you young Democrats. I couldn't stand the tension.

Sure. Sure. You're all saying, look at Sheila Levine —says she's a liberal, fights for blacks to move into white neighborhoods, but would she kiss one?

Madeline, you in your little house in Franklin Square, so what would you do? Sure, I know, you were all for busing blacks, but are you all for kissing blacks? That is the question.

Mom, speak up for your generation. Admit it. You want me married more than life. But! You think—better single than integrated.

So Thomas Brown (I always think it's embarrassing when a brown person is named Brown) sat next to me. (He was the one in pinstripes.) What do you talk about? Suppose he's from Harlem. I don't want to bring up any horrible memories. . . . So, where'd you go to school? . . . No, can't say that. Suppose he didn't go to school. I don't want to embarrass him. . . . So, what do you do? . . . Can't. Suppose he went to school but, because of his color, he couldn't get a job suited to his education. I couldn't talk to this person. My own hang-up. Yeah. . . . And the hang-up of the rest of the world.

"Is this your first time here?"

"Yes." (That's all I could think of to say.)

"What're you here for? Looking for a good lay?"

Now, if Thomas Brown were white, I would have sneered. Not done anything dramatic like slapped, but I would have sneered. Since he was black and I was very afraid of hurting his feelings lest he would feel I wasn't a friend of the black people, I smiled. Did you ever do that? Accept from a black person what you wouldn't accept from a white because you're so afraid of hurting them. Oh, boy, are we prejudiced and we don't know it.

So Martha suggests we all go back to my place since I live closest, and once again, I can't refuse. You see, to me, I am refusing to have the entire black race at my home if I refuse Mr. Brown. I say yes, and I really don't like him. He's saying things like "fuck" in my ear.

Back to my place. Martha Katz and Herman Freemont together in one chair. Thomas Brown and Sheila

Levine on the couch. Still nothing to talk about. I was afraid to ask questions. Really afraid of saying something wrong.

This was the first time I had a black person in my home. It was strange. I'm not going to lie and say it wasn't. I kept thinking over and over again that he was black and my bedspread is black and, look, isn't that interesting, my light switch is black. Black, and if you want to really know the truth (and I haven't lied so far), black and not so beautiful.

He reached for my hand. I let him hold my hand. Not that I wanted him to hold my hand, but the same old problem—if I don't let him hold my hand, will he think that I'm prejudiced? We all watched the *Tonight Show*. Lena Horne was on, and I kept thinking she's black and he's black, and what do you know about that?

That goddamn Martha and her goddamn pickup left. Left me alone—with him. I swear to God on a stack of Bibles, cross my heart and hope to die (cute), if he were white, I would have kicked him out. He was obnoxious.

"You one of them chicks who's always looking for a good lay?"

"No."

"How'd you like to have one?"

"No thank you. I mean, not now."

"What's the matter, baby? Is it because I'm black?"

"No, of course not. I'm not that type of person. I don't care whether a person is black or white or green or red or blue or purple or orange. It doesn't matter to me at all. We are all people, equal people, and that's what counts. I really don't care what the color of a man's skin is."

"And what about a good lay? Don't you like a good lay?"

"Sure I do. I like a good lay as much as the next

145

person." (He had me and he knew he had me and I didn't know how to get out of it. Would you, Mrs. Liberal? Come on, Madeline, the girl comes in every Thursday; would you have her brother come in on Friday nights when the hubby is out of town?)

"Come here, baby."

And I went there and, okay, we did it. It wasn't bad, but it wasn't good either. Don't ask me if black men are bigger. I didn't look. Thomas Brown took advantage of me. He knew that Jewish girl Sheila Levine didn't want to look prejudiced. He knew that if he played his cards right, I would sleep with him in the name of civil rights. That wasn't fair, Thomas Brown. How many good Thursday nights did you have with girls who went to Friday's? If you were white, I would have thrown you out.

Calm down. Calm down, everyone. What I am about to tell you is probably going to shock you. As a matter of fact, Mother, I would, if I were you, take a Librium before I went on.

"Manny, what more could she possibly say that's going to shock me more than she's shocked me already?"

I had an abortion.

"Manny, did you read that? Look, Sheila had an abortion! Manny, I can't breathe—bring me my pills."

I had an abortion in the days when it wasn't legal in New York. In the good old days of flying down to Puerto Rico or driving to New Jersey.

I didn't have to have the abortion. I could have had the child. Raised it. Girls do that, you know. I didn't have the strength.

Actually, I always thought that I'd have a child at thirty-five whether I was married or not.

FACT: Most single girls plan to have a child when

146

they're thirty-five whether they're married or not . . . and never do.

The prospect of actually planning for a fatherless child is indeed very interesting. You'd want the best possible genes—like a John Lennon maybe. If it's your husband, you're willing to take the wavy-hair genes. If you're out there picking, you might as well have the best. The depressing fact is—I can't think of anyone I've slept with who I'd like to be the absentee father of my child. Let's face it. The guys I've slept with don't have great genes.

"Norman, you know we fool around a lot. Suppose that something happens."

"Whadda you mean?"

"I mean, suppose that I became pregnant or something."

"Are you pregnant?"

"No, I don't think so." (Yes, I think so.)

"So why are we doing all this supposing?"

"Why can't we just suppose every once in a while? God damn it, Norman, everyone supposes. WHY CAN'T WE SUPPOSE? GIVE ME ONE GOOD REASON."

"All right. So we'll suppose. What do you want to suppose?"

"I want to suppose I'm pregnant."

"So suppose you're pregnant?"

"What would happen?"

"I don't know what would happen. What do you want to happen?"

"I don't know."

"Are we through supposing?"

"No, we're not. If I were pregnant, what would we do? Get rid of it?"

"Get rid of the pregnancy?"

"Yeah. Get rid of the kid. Is that what you want?"

"I don't know."

147

"Would you rather get married or something?"

"I don't know."

"Why don't you know?"

No help from Norman. You wanna know the truth? I didn't know if the little baby inside me was the son of Norman Berkowitz or Thomas Brown. Yeah . . . yeah . . . yeah. I counted the days. It could have been the son of Thomas Brown. Not that I didn't use the diaphragm that night. I always used the diaphragm. Somebody's sperm snuck past the little rubber cup and my bet was, considering how sneaky he was, that it was Thomas Brown's. Actually, Thomas Jr. would definitely be a cuter baby than Norman Jr.

(My mother) "Isn't it the cutest thing in the world? They're so cute when they're little."

(Norman) "Sheila, did you see the baby? I think they made a mistake when they labeled him or something."

(The doctor) "Mrs. Berkowitz, you have a fine boy there. We will, in addition to your husband's name, need the name of the real father for our records."

"My husband is the real father."

"Come, Mrs. Berkowitz. We're not stupid, you know."

And, oh, the relatives and the whispering. I mean, it's very easy to fool Norman, but I'm sure even he would catch on eventually.

I wasn't feeling very maternal, and I didn't feel that I was destroying a life. The abortion seemed like the easiest way out. A lot of girls had them, you know. Friend after friend after friend. Very common, those abortions were.

It really wasn't a dirty garage or anything like that. Just a nice doctor, New Paltz, New York, recommended by Martha Katz, who had used him twice. Just a nice doctor who believed in that sort of thing. I was scared they were going to slap him in jail while I lay

148

bleeding on the table. Some pain, five hundred dollars, and the product of my love was down the drain.

Regrets? Yeah. Relief? Yeah. Did I ever look back and wish I had had the kid? Yeah. Was I ever glad that I did it? Yeah.

Wanna know what I really felt badly about? New York is so abortion-minded, it's part of the culture, and yet they passed that abortion bill too late for the hundreds of girls who needed abortions when I did. Couldn't they have made it retroactive and written us all an apology?

Cosmopolitan magazine has dirty horoscopes. They also have great articles on masturbation.

Did you ever have your chart done? So what's your rising sign? Twenty-five bucks. You can be satisfied for just so long with your monthly forecasts in magazines, daily forecasts in newspapers. To Mrs. Alberta Kile I went to learn about my future.

"You will have a long, happy life."

"Will I be married?"

"Your chart indicates that you can be, but probably not between your thirty-fourth and forty-first year. See, Venus is nowhere near you then."

"What about before that or after that? Huh?"

"It's hard to say. Your chart is very complicated. You will have career satisfaction later on in life."

"Will I get married?"

"You could."

"Will I?"

"Your chart seems to indicate a long attachment with a man."

"And marriage?"

"Possibly."

"Don't you see marriage in my chart?"

"Yes and no. Not between thirty-four and forty-one. Possibly before or after."

"Can't you tell for sure?"

"Sometimes. Sometimes it's very obvious. Not with your chart. Don't fly on the twentieth."

Oh, fuck off, Mrs. Kile. Why'd you take my twenty-five dollars and then tell me dumb things about flying? Christ.

A long attachment with a man? Norman. He was the longest attachment I had ever had. I did meet this other teacher at the school, Alfred Block. We dated, had a short affair—all before I learned there was a Mrs. Alfred Block, two children and a dog. We were in bed one night. (On a non-Norman night.)

"Sheila, could you hand me my pants? [I reached over and got them. He pulled out his wallet and showed me some pictures.] And here's Jennifer, she's two and a half; Sean, he's seven now; and Adam, he's five."

"They're adorable." (I was plotzing. It was a good thing I was lying down or I would have fallen down.)

"And here's a picture of my wife, Barbara."

"She's very pretty."

Alfred Block, you're a prick. You never told me you were married. How many girls didn't you tell? And, oh, what a lovely way to finally tell somebody. In bed, after fucking—"and this is my wife, Barbara." Alfred Block, you're a cunt. Is that possible?

He was the only married man I ever dated. Wait a minute . . . not true. There was a Bernie something, but that really didn't count because he hated his wife and he told me some of the things she did to him and I hated her too. His wife hadn't slept with him in more than a month, claiming she had headaches so that didn't really count . . . did it?

Norman didn't know about the Bernies and the Alfreds, and he was faithful to me. Like a little old married man afraid to cheat on his wife. No, probably not even afraid. More fucking just wasn't on his schedule.

Now that we were both teaching, we had the same schedules, and Norman and I went, one Easter vacation, to Puerto Rico—as man and wife. Sin. Sin. We sinned in the Caribe Hilton.

It was fun. Not exciting fun, but fun considering whom I was with. Gave me a taste of what being married to Norman would be really like. Just like it always sounded. It would be, in fact, being married to dirty water. He forgot to make reservations, forgot to leave tips, and wore baggy swimming trunks—are you ready? —with flecks.

Despite all this, I was willing to marry him. Yeah, marry him and have his children and buy his lox. So he dresses funny. I'll buy him new clothes. Do everything for him that Bernice did for Manny. Look here, world, this is my husband—dirty water.

So I finally proposed. The night before we left Puerto Rico.

"Norman, I really think we're wasting each others time if we don't get married."

"I don't think so."

(And I gambled with love . . .) "Then I really think we should stop seeing each other."

"Okay." (. . . and lost.)

Hey! All you lawyers out there. You wanna hear a great idea? I think girls who have really been going with guys for a long time and have really given a lot of themselves to the guy should be able to collect alimony. If that ever happened, more single guys would think twice about screwing up a girl's whole life. I dated Norman for like seven, eight years. Some wives get alimony after being married seven, eight months. Yeah, alimony for dating.

Just like that—"Okay"—a seven-year thing down the toilet. Flushed away in the night. (Such imagery.) "Okay," he says, and that was the end of it.

I talked to Norman again, asked, begged him to come back, but his schedule had changed.

And what's left to tell? I was robbed again. They took the television and the fur coat. I should have had the nose job. You can't steal a nose job. Melissa had a baby—a girl. Aunt Sheila went to visit. I read in *The NYU Alumni News* that Professor Hinley is now teaching at Miami University. I hope he has found another Joshua. At twenty-eight, I cancelled my subscription to *Mademoiselle* and ordered *Vogue* for the more mature woman. I started thinking about saving money and wondering who was going to take care of me in my old age. My niece?

Kate got married. A chic little affair at the Fifth Avenue Hotel. Both sets of parents were there. (Kate married well.) Last I heard from Linda, she was floating around Europe. I got a card from Denmark and a card from England—"Just broke up with a real weird one. He digs the queen." Agatha Horowitz's marriage announcement was in the Sunday *Times*.

I didn't go to my high school reunion because I didn't want to run into a lot of pregnant classmates. And the closer I got to thirty, the harder it was to get laid. Could it be? I was no longer a sex object? A few men felt me on the street, but it wasn't at all satisfying. I tried going to women's lib meetings, but women's lib and I just didn't jell. You know, I liked what they were saying, but it didn't make me any happier. I could change my name from Miss Levine to Ms. Levine, and it wouldn't help. I have no idea where Joshua is. He probably ended up with Norman.

And it was . . . Happy birthday to you
Happy birthday to you
Happy birthday, dear unmarried Sheila
Happy birthday to you, and many more.

No, no more.

That was my mother and father singing to me on my thirtieth birthday in the Four Seasons. Just the three of us.

"Sheila, dear, I've been thinking—and I even mentioned this to your father. Maybe the reason you're not married is because you're too fussy. Like why does he have to be a college graduate?"

I tried that, Mom . . . Marty Brink, the noncollege grad. Marty was in ladies' shoes. Went right from high school into his father's business. I went out with him a few times, and eventually, as was the custom of the times, we hit the sack together. Right after we had intercourse the first time, Marty, still atop me, said, "I'm sorry, Sheila, I shouldn't have came." You wanna talk about turnoffs? I get sick when I think about it. Sorry, Mom, you shouldn't have sent me to college. I should have gone to typing school.

And I thought to myself—ENOUGH ALREADY, I'M GOING TO COMMIT SUICIDE.

Why enough already? Because I'm not married, that's why. I NEVER GOT CLEAN WATER! Call it one woman's answer to the population explosion. What better way to practice ecology than to dispose of yourself?

Actually, there was one alternative to taking my own life. If only I could have been a *Glamour* make-over. I wrote to them, and they never answered. I considered it an omen. Suicide became the only answer.

My past and present meet, and there is no future. My parents took me out to my birthday dinner shortly before I started writing this note.

Do you realize the planning that goes into a death? Probably even more than goes into a marriage. This, after all, really is for eternity.

Arrangements

YOU CAN'T IMAGINE how great I felt once I made the decision. I know it's strange, but I felt healthy. You don't know what a relief it is to finally ignore Dr. Stillman and his water diet, to say good-bye to Dr. Atkins and his low carbohydrates. Now I didn't even have to consider getting those pregnant women's urine shots. True. They help you lose weight. Yes, sir, the first thing I did when I made the decision to kill myself was to stop dieting. Let them dig a wider hole.

My whole attitude was different. I started wearing plaid pleated skirts. I wore diagonal stripes and unslenderizing colors. I took cabs everywhere and didn't worry about the meter. I went to Broadway shows and sat in the orchestra. It's hard to believe that Jackie Onassis did those things without thinking twice.

Impending suicide improved my personality. Really, I became more honest, more direct and perhaps a little devil-may-care. I even became a better teacher because I stopped being afraid one of the kids was going to kill me with a switchblade knife.

Most people, I imagine, plan to commit suicide and then just go out and do it. I couldn't do that. It's so tacky. New York had taught me some class and I was going to go in style. Not like in *Imitation of Life* with six white horses drawing my casket. Nice and quiet, as elegant as possible, and planned out to every detail.

I made the decision in late August and intended to carry the whole thing off by July 3 of the next year. That way, I would have time to buy a plot, a tombstone, and, of course, to write a suicide note. You're asking why July 3? So maybe you're not asking, but I'm going to tell you anyway. I figured if I kill myself July 3, I'll have to be buried on the fourth. Isn't that nice and symbolic? July 4—my private Independence Day.

I know it's silly but way back in August, I bought a rubber stamp that said DECEASED. I saw this ad in the back of the *New York Times Magazine* section one Sunday that said, "We'll put anything on a rubber stamp, Especially Good for Business Purposes," or something like that. I couldn't resist. At first I wanted it to say "Fuck Off." I thought that would look great stamped on my rent bill, but I didn't have the guts. Anyway, Mom—Dad, and anyone else who will be taking care of my effects—stamp DECEASED on my library card. Stamp it on my unpaid bills.

You know, I never thought of it before—suppose a person got a monstrous bill from Lord & Taylor because that person couldn't control herself at a great end-of-the-season sale. Why couldn't the person just send back the bill with a polite little note telling how the person was deceased? What would happen? I suppose they could check it out and send a bill collector, but the person who was billed could wear black and pretend to be in mourning for a few months after the note was sent. It would be worth it. Lord & Taylor has some great end-of-the-season sales.

In any case, Dad, you will find the rubber stamp reading DECEASED in the top drawer of my desk.

"Did you hear? The Levine girl killed herself."

"What a horrible thing to do to her parents."

"She arranged for the whole funeral and bought her own plot and tombstone and everything."

"I should be so lucky with my own children."

I have my plot. Believe me, it was not easy to come by. I decided in order to make it easier for my parents who, according to Jewish law, would have to visit my grave at least once a year, to be buried at Rossman Memorial Park, where my grandparents (two on my father's side, one on my mother's), they should rest in peace, were buried. My family does own a plot out at Rossman's, but there's only room for my mother and father and my aunt and uncle. Grandchildren are on their own.

I took a bus out to South Orange, New Jersey, and then a cab to the cemetery. A quiet day. A few people milling, one or two rabbis looking for work. (They get paid by the family for saying a prayer graveside.)

I was always embarrassed by cemeteries. Whenever I entered one, I bowed my head, afraid to look the mourners in the eye. Not any longer. The cemetery is now merely a place to hang my hat, so to speak. It's like looking at a new apartment and, thank God, I won't have to move again.

I visited my grandparents, said a few words, envied them for being together and let them know I'd be joining them soon. Then on to the cemetery office.

"May I help you?" (A lady dressed in black, gray hair, one simple pin and a lot of sympathy.)

"I'd like to arrange for a plot."

"Won't you sit down?"

The lady went into an office and returned with a tall, all-gray man, who very solemnly invited me into his office. Such nice, concerned people. I wonder if I told them why I was killing myself if they would find me a man.

He sat me down in a chair, made sure I was comfortable and that there was a box of Kleenex next to me. Then he sat down in another chair, not behind his desk, but facing me. Good eye contact.

156

"Mrs. Goldman told me you were looking for a plot. Do you know anything about Rossman Memorial Park?"

"My grandparents are buried here."

"That's nice."

"Do you have any plots left?"

"Yes, we do. We have some wonderful plots. Some even have a view." (A view?)

"I just want something simple."

"May I ask who it's for?"

"For me. I have this terminal illness. Nothing serious. I mean, you can't catch it or anything, but I'll be needing a plot."

He got up and came back with some sort of portfolio. He opened it and turned the pages quickly. He looked up once, and I smiled. He didn't smile back. I guess those people are trained not to smile. Finally, his eyes rested on a page.

(Showing me a map) "Here we are. We have site Thirty-four A and B and we have site Sixty-five A and B. They're both lovely locations."

"What do A and B mean?"

"A and B are two plots together. I assume your husband will be joining us."

"I'm single." (That's why I'm going to be here, shmuck!)

"That is a problem. A very serious problem. [He's telling me!] You see, Rossman Memorial Park is a family cemetery. We have the Linbergers, over twenty-five members, three generations, with us. The problem is, dear, we don't cater to single people. All our plots are double."

Do you believe it? Do you believe what this man is saying to me? Rest in peace. Ha! To my grave, in my grave, I'm having single problems.

"Couldn't I . . . couldn't I just have site Thirty-four

157

A and if someone else single comes in, they could have Thirty-four B?"

"I'm sorry. I can't break them up. It'll throw us all off." (I'm ready to cry. I'm ready to scream. I'm ready to die!)

"Look, maybe a man died and his wife remarried and she's gonna want to be with her new husband. Maybe a woman died and the husband remarried and he's gonna want to be with his new wife. Maybe there's another single girl lying around somewhere and we could team up, if you allow that sort of thing."

"What we usually do, Miss Levine, is suggest that single people be cremated." Don't we even have a choice? Are we that unimportant? Must single people be reduced to ashes whether they want to or not?

"I don't want to be cremated." (I start to get up and leave.)

"Tell you what, Miss Levine, I'll give you site Sixty-five A and B for only slightly more than it would cost you for one. It's on a slight hill. Is that okay?"

"Fine."

"Now, about a casket."

"Don't, please don't tell me you only have double caskets (or queen-sized or king-sized)." He almost smiled, but he didn't. He must have had great training.

"No, we have caskets for you. That is, if you're sure you'd rather not be in an urn."

"I'm sure. Look, can I call you on the casket?" I had a certain amount of money put away for the casket and the dress I was to be buried in. You know, if I spent less on the dress, I could spend more on the casket. I didn't know how much I was going to have left over at this point.

"Fine. Here's my card. Just be sure you send in a deposit of, let's say, a hundred and fifty dollars. Our plots go quickly." I was sure he was going to tell me there is a nice couple really interested in the one I just bought, and I half expected him to tell me I should take the plot because it had charming alcoves.

So I'm going to spend my eternity at Rossman's, a single girl, alone, in a double plot.

So do you happen to know anybody in the wholesale tombstone business? Neither did I.

One fine Saturday morning not long ago, I set out to buy myself a gravestone. Every grave needs its stone, and I had my grave. It was now time to get my stone. I was at first letting my fingers do the walking through the Yellow Pages, writing down friendly-sounding gravestone companies: Granite Memorials, Specializing in Images; and Lodge Memorials, serving Jewish Families Since 1915; and Miguel Rodriguez, Se Habla Español. Nothing really hit me. Raynd Jones & Associates, MEMORIAL COUNSELORS. Memorial counselors? Yeah, memorial counselors. I guess they counseled memorials.

"Son, when you grow up, I want you to go into the memorial counseling business. I think it has a great future."

So where do I go? Specializing in Images . . . nah! I would have considered them if I had had the nose job. All of a sudden it hit me—Bingo Memorials.

Bingo Memorials is in Connecticut—Kent, Connecticut. I saw Bingo's twice a year when I was young, once going up to camp, once coming home from camp. A very strange place, Bingo's was. There was a little house, white and run-down, and the whole front yard was full of gravestones.

I always saw children, lots of dirty, blond children, playing around the house, watching the buses taking us to camp. Those children leaned on, sat on, played among tombstones all day long. While we were in camp, swimming and trying to play tennis (keep your wrist straight, Sheila, how many times do I have to tell

159

you to keep your wrist straight?), these children played in their front yard, crowded with memorials. I felt so sorry for those children. They didn't get to go to camp. Probably didn't go to college. But, Sheila, they got married—those lucky, lucky kids.

To Franklin Square . . .

"Hello, Mom."

"Hi, Sheila, what's new?"

"Nothing much."

"Are you going out Saturday night?" (She was still trying.)

"I don't know yet." (And I was still trying to please her.)

"When are you coming home for the weekend?"

"I don't know, Mom. I'll be home the first chance I get. [She must have thought I was Baby Jane Holzer.] Listen, Mom, could I borrow the car on Saturday?"

"Where are you going?" (Mom, for God's sake, I'm thirty years old. Can't I once borrow the car without telling you where I'm going?)

"I'm going up to Connecticut to Bingo Memorials to pick out my gravestone." (I didn't say that.)

I did say: "I'm going up to Connecticut with this boy I met a few weeks ago. He said he loves Connecticut and I said I love Connecticut, so we're going up there just for the day." (I knew by now exactly the right thing to say.)

"Very nice. Why don't the *two* of you come out here first and pick up the car?" (She wanted a look-see at my fictitious beau.)

"He would love to come, Mom, but he can't."

"Why not?"

"Because he doesn't really exist. I made him up." (I didn't say that either.)

I did say: "Because he has to visit his mother on Saturday morning." (I knew my mother couldn't yet compete with his mother.)

160

"Okay, so we'll see you when?"

"Saturday morning, I'll come out and pick up the car."

"Why not Friday night? We're having a nice Friday night dinner." (Why'd you ask me when I'm coming if you're telling me when I'm coming?)

"Okay."

I drove by myself to Kent, Connecticut—two and a half hours of beautiful America. It was my first trip to old familiar grounds by car. Year after year after year, I made the trip up by train with gum-chewing, comic-holding bunkmates in navy shorts and light blue polo shirts. We took the train to the station at Kent and then were picked up by buses and trucks to take us the rest of the way.

On this fine Saturday morning, I went directly to Bingo's and was surprised not to see children there. I had completely forgotten that the children who played there were my age and had grown up too.

I knocked on the door. It was immediately opened by a lady—Mrs. Bingo?—in a housedress. In my whole life I never really knew anybody who wore housedresses. Mrs. Bingo had long, thin hair that was graying, wore housedresses and was the type that didn't put on weight.

(Me, very friendly and smiley) "Hello, I'm here to see about a monument."

(She, very curious) "Wait here. I'll get my husband. You wait."

I peeked inside. Shabby, well-worn furniture, ripped and torn and crawled on by children. No two pieces matched. The whole place looked like an old, cheap motel lobby. A television set, old and dusty, with a new *TV Guide* on top. A man appeared. And what does the husband of a woman who wears housedresses look like? He was tall and thin and wore socks with clocks and Gucci shoes—I'm kidding about the shoes.

161

(Me, very, very friendly and smiley) "Hello, I'm here to see about a monument."

He looked at me—a look that said, "What the hell are you doing *here?*"

"I used to go to camp near here and I always noticed your place and I need a tombstone, so I thought I'd come here."

"There's our stones. You pick what you like, and then you come to me and I'll write it up."

"Thank you."

And I looked at the stones. Do you know? Do you have any idea what those tombstones looked like? They were tombstones for married people. Hearts and flowers and angels and words like "IN MEMORY OF MY BE-LOVED WIFE," "MY BELOVED HUSBAND," "BELOVED WIFE AND MOTHER." Oh, God, even the monuments were for married people. There was an occasional "OUR BELOVED CHILD" but they all had crosses atop them.

(Me, friendlier and more smiley than ever) "Mr. Bingo, do you happen to make gravestones to special order?"

(After a pause) "Them there is made to order. You tell us the name you want and we put it in there."

"No, I mean completely to order. Like you start from scratch. There's nothing written on it at all."

He pointed to a blank one—in the form of a large cross with two tiny angels resting at the bottom. (Oh, boy!)

"Yes, that's very nice, but what I wanted, what I really had in mind, was a perfectly plain stone—nothing on it."

"How you gonna know who's buried there if there ain't nothin' on it?"

"No, what I mean is, could you take a perfectly plain slab and write on it what I want to write on it?"

"You can write on these here." (He pointed to all the beloved memorials.)

"Those aren't any good for my purpose. You see, the person wasn't a beloved wife or mother."

"Sorry, I can't be of help."

"Thanks anyway."

I drove up to camp. There was a rope across the road with a sign reading NO TRESPASSING. I moved the rope aside and drove in. That's something I never would have done before "the decision." I was always the type who's afraid of the principal. My dear mother always used to say, "Why should you be afraid of anyone, Sheila? Just picture whoever you're afraid of sitting on the toilet."

Camps don't change. That's a very good thing to know in our ever-changing world. It was cold, and I had never been there in the cold, but it looked like camp. What happy times I spent there. I can almost forget I was so unathletic that when my bunkmates chose up teams, I was always last to be chosen. Every day I heard, "You've got Sheila."

So, back in New York I called Raynd Jones and Associates, MEMORIAL COUNSELORS. It turns out they were actually in the same business as Mr. Bingo; only they sent me a catalog and a fast-talking salesman. He wore a pinky ring and a tie tack. Where do the rich get gravestones? Surely not from this man.

"Whom, may I ask, is the memorial for?"

"It's for myself. I have this terminal disease."

"I'm sorry to hear that, but I'm happy you came to Raynd Jones and Associates, Memorial Counselors."

"Yes, I'd like something simple."

"Here is our catalog. Why don't you take a peek at it?"

A catalog for beloved wives and mothers. There are no single monuments. "What I wanted was something simple. All I want my gravestone to say is, 'HERE LIES SHEILA LEVINE, BELOVED WIFE OF NO ONE.' Can you do that?"

"Are you crazy, lady? Do you realize all that work is done by hand? The engraving is five dollars a letter. Are you sure you need all those letters?"

"Yes."

"Let's see now, for a real small stone, that'll run you five times—let's see—five times thirty-eight, that's zero, carry the four. That's one ninety for the engraving and, let's say one fifty for the stone—real small but marble —that's zero, nine and five are fourteen. Approximately three forty, three fifty, let's say, payable in advance."

"Okay."

"Where and when do you want it delivered?"

"It has to be finished around July fourth because I plan to die on July third and be buried on the fourth."

"I see." (He wrote that information down.)

"And why don't you deliver it here?"

"Too heavy, your whole floor will cave in."

"I'll let you know where. Can you bill me?"

"I can bill you, but I'll need, say, a hundred-dollar deposit to get this in the works."

I wrote out a check. Damn it! I'll bet Rose Lehman's sister knows somebody who could get it for me wholesale.

My life has not been one of simple pleasure, right? I don't need any aggravation, right? I keep getting aggravation. Right.

From Franklin Square. . . .

"Hello, Sheila, darling, did I wake you?"

I looked at my alarm clock. "Mom, it's six thirty."

"I can't sleep. The minute the light hits the window, I'm up. I don't know how I function with such little sleep."

All I know is the woman is in bed at tĕn o'clock at night. She is the only person in America who doesn't know who Johnny Carson is.

"Sheila, darling, how are you?"

164

"Fine, Mom." (I'm about to kill myself in a little over six months, but it's still "Fine, Mom.")

"Do you remember Great-Aunt Goldie, Uncle Arnie's mother?"

"No."

"You do so remember. She was the one always used to get in the center when they were doing the hora at weddings."

"I don't remember."

"Yes, you do. Uncle Arnie's mother. She knit you a sweater when you were born."

"Ma, how am I supposed to remember someone who knit me a sweater when I was born?"

"Don't be so fresh! She's the one who used to take a place in Atlantic City every summer."

"Oh, yeah." (I had no idea who she was talking about.)

"You remember her?"

"Yeah." (No)

"She died."

My mother is crying for Aunt Goldie, whom she hardly knows (Atlantic City and the hora). What will she do for me? What will you do, Mom? Don't cry. It's what I want. I've had enough of life, and I did what I wanted to do. Be happy! Go to a movie. Don't sit shiva for Sheila. It's what she wanted. Dad, don't cry and don't let Mom cry. Is there a guilt after death?

Did you have a feeling that Aunt Goldie's death was going to be trouble? It was.

From Franklin Square. . . .

"Sheila?"

"Yes, Mom." (How many times have I said that in a life-time?)

"Uncle Arnie can't come in from San Francisco in time to make the funeral arrangements. The funeral has to be right away, not like the goyim who leave the

165

bodies around for days. [I know, I know. I go July 3. I go under July 4.] So that leaves me to make the funeral arrangements because I'm the closest relative. I'm going to make arrangements at Rossman's. That's where Great-Aunt Goldie's husband is, and that's where Grandma and Grandpa are buried. [I know. I know.] Please, Sheila, could you drive me out to Rossman's this afternoon? I can't ask your father to because this is his busy season. Please, Sheila, darling, drive me out to Rossman's."

AND YOU THINK YOU HAVE PROBLEMS!

How do I get through this? How do I come face to face with those gray people, whom I had met only a few weeks before to make my *own* funeral arrangements? Maybe they won't recognize me. Of course, they'll recognize you. How many people come in to buy their own plots? Maybe the man who helped me won't be there. I can't take the chance. He may be there *and* the woman may be there. Maybe I won't have to get out of the car. No. My mother will get me out of the car—to stretch my legs, to go to the bathroom, to visit my grandparents' grave. Say hello to Grandma and Grandpa. . . . "Please, Sheila, darling, come with me. I'll feel so much better if you're there." So maybe I'd better call the gray people and try to explain. What's his name? Her name was Mrs. Goldman. Thank God I had inscribed her name in my suicide note.

"Information, Rossman Memorial Park, South Orange, New Jersey. Thank you, operator."

"Hello, Rossman's Memorial Park."

"Hello, is Mrs. Goldman there?"

"Mrs. Goldman is out of town. She's coming back with the bereaved family." (Shit!)

"Can I please speak to the man who Mrs. Goldman works for?"

166

"Which one? She works for all of the Rossman brothers." (The gray one. Are they all gray?)

"I don't remember his name, but I have to speak to him. It's very, very important."

"My other phone is ringing. Can I put you on hold?" (My mother is rolling into the city to pick me up and I'm on hold. ON HOLD! In heaven, you get right through. In hell, they put you on hold.)

"Hello?"

"Yes, I'm still here."

"Could you describe the gentleman to me?"

"He has gray hair and sort of grayish skin and gray eyes, I think." (And gray socks and gray shoes and gray ears, nose and throat.)

"I'll put you through to Mr. Henry Rossman." (Please God, I'm praying. Jesus, I'll convert if this is the right man.)

"Hello?"

"Hello, this is Sheila Levine. I don't know if I spoke to you or not, but I was at your cemetery a few weeks ago to buy myself a plot. Did I speak to you about it? Remember, I bought two plots, Sixty-five A and B, I think. Remember, I'm the single girl?"

"Ah, yes, I remember." (Thank God—I was only kidding, Jesus.)

"Thank God."

"How are you, Miss Levine?" (I was the one with the terminal illness, shmuck! So how should I be a few short months before I die?)

"Fine."

"Good." (He didn't mean "Good." He meant, "That's too bad." I think he was afraid that I was calling because I'd gotten well and was canceling Sixty-five A and B.)

"I'm calling because I'm coming out there today and I'll probably see you and I don't want you to recognize me."

"What?"

"My mother's aunt died and she's going to be buried at Rossman's and I'm coming out there today with my mother and I'd appreciate it if you would make believe you don't know me because my mother doesn't know that I'm very sick and that I'll be joining you soon. So I would appreciate it if you would not know me this afternoon. Please!"

"Why don't you tell your mother you're dying? I think she could help you, Sheila." (Please, tall gray man, please, no long-distance lectures.)

"I'm going to tell her, but I'm waiting for exactly the right moment." (Good thinking, girl.)

"I see. I guess you know what you're doing." (I have no idea what I'm doing, but I'm glad you guess I know.)

"Yes. I have it all thought out."

"See you later then. And don't worry. I'll pretend I never saw you."

"Good. And please tell Mrs. Goldman not to recognize me either."

"Mrs. Goldman is out of town with a bereaved family."

"Good . . . I didn't exactly mean that."

"Miss Levine, I never asked you if you wanted care for the grave."

"Oh, yes. Yes, I do." I didn't care how much it cost. I wasn't taking any chances that he'd go back on his word and recognize me.

I met my mother on Thirty-eighth because Thirty-ninth is a one-way street going in the wrong direction. That's generally how New Yorkers live. They plan out every move they have to make because they're constantly thinking of what streets go in what direction. My mother pulled up, I got behind the wheel, and Mother slid over as if choreographed. A perfect ren-

168

dezvous. For the first ten minutes, she was abnormally quiet. Then:

"Well, we've all got to go sometime. Aunt Goldie had a good, full life. And the way she died—that was a blessing. That's the way I want to go—a quick heart attack. It's a blessing. I hope I go before your father. That's my one wish, that I get a heart attack and go before your father. It's a terrible thing being a widow. Look at Frances Lehman. Since her Herman died, she's been depressed. That's not for me. Frances has three daughters, all married, so they all have their own lives. They don't have time for Frances. She went around the world by herself last year. That's a life? Don't let them put me in an old age home, Sheila. Look what they did to Louise Schnitzer's mother. I hear they hit her in that old age home. I couldn't stay with Melissa. She's got her own life. Maybe I'll come live with you, Sheila. Would you like that—living with your old mother? To look at me, you'd never know that I was once Miss Coney Island. I had so many boyfriends. I almost married what's-his-name, the bandleader. It's terrible to get old. Do I have a lot of wrinkles? I mean, for a woman of my age? Maybe it was a good thing you never got married, Sheila. If anything, God forbid, ever happened to your father, I could move in with you. I'm glad I had daughters—you can always rely on them."

All my life she wanted me to get married. Now she wants me to stay single so she can live with me when she has no teeth. I thought, "Next time I go to Rossman's, it's going to be in a box. A lot more pleasant than this trip."

It seems, in case you hadn't heard, that Henry Rossman is not a great actor. The minute he saw me, his face turned grayish red. He coughed. He stuttered. He tripped. He did everything that a man who accidentally met his mistress when he was with his wife would do. Overacted.

"Hello, Miss Levine. Nice to meet you." (A big "Nice to meet you" with a wink yet.)

"Hello."

"Miss Levine, would you like to look around? I know you've never been here before." (Don't be stupid, Henry. And now, the award for the worst actor of the year. The nominees are Henry Rossman.)

"Your aunt will rest next to her husband. He's in plot Sixty-three A. She'll be in Sixty-three B, right near —whoops." (Oh, Henry, you putz, you shmuck, you male organ, you.)

"Would you like to see the plot, Mrs. Levine, and would you like to come, Miss Levine?" (I'm surprised he didn't say, "Would you like to come, Miss . . . excuse me, I've forgotten your name because I've never seen you before. Would you like to come and see the plot and take a peek at where you'll be buried? Whoops!")

We looked at the plot—I don't know why. They weren't going to move Aunt Goldie's husband, so why look? Back in Henry Rossman's office, Henry turned psychiatrist. Dumb Henry decided that he was going to create the right moment for me to tell my mother about my horrible disease. Are you ready for this? Neither was I.

"How old was your aunt, Mrs. Levine?"

"Ninety-one."

"Do you know our average age here is sixty-one. We are very proud of that." (What the hell is that supposed to mean?)

"That's nice." (Either my mother said that or I said that. We were both confused and I had long ago begun talking like my mother.)

"So your aunt was ninety-one? She led a long, full life. When a person of that age goes, it's sad, but not

170

as sad as when a young person goes. When a young person goes, it's sad, very sad, especially if that young person is sick and doesn't tell her family about it."

"We better be going, Mother. You'll have to drive all the way back to Long Island and you don't want to get into any traffic on the way. LET'S GO, MOTHER!"

He went on, raising eyebrows, opening spots for me to open my heart.

"I think young people should talk about their problems. . . ." (Pause.)

"Sheila, you look like a bright girl. Even though I've never laid eyes on you before, I could tell that. Don't you think that if a young person is sick and going to die that they should talk it over with their parents. . . . [Pause.] I know of a young girl who is going to die and she hasn't told her parents about it. I would like to give her some advice. What do you think I should tell her to do, Sheila?"

Finally, escape to the car. My mother told me she thought Henry Rossman was strange, and I told her the funeral business probably did that to him, and she had seen *The Loved One*, so she accepted my answer.

The funeral was the next day, and everybody kept talking about what a full life Aunt Goldie led. She had a happy life—got to dance at her son's wedding. I'm sure it was very full. Born in Brooklyn, died in Brooklyn, had one son who moved to San Francisco, two grandchildren whom she got to hug once in a while when she went west, and a trip to Miami every winter. She also had a eulogy. A eulogy said by a rabbi who never met her.

"I never met Goldie Butkin, but I know she was a wonderful woman, for this woman was a MOTHER. A MOTHER. [He pointed in the direction of Goldie's son.] A MOTHER is . . . a MOTHER is . . . like the COVER of a BOOK. The family is the book, BUT the MOTHER is the cover. I ask you, if the COVER of the

171

BOOK, which is the MOTHER, gets worn and old, does that mean that the BOOK, which is the family, is no good? NO! The BOOK, which is the FAMILY, is still GOOD because the MOTHER has protected it. . . . What you do is take the cover off and throw it away . . . but do you take the mother off . . . no. . . . Maybe the mother is not like the cover of a book . . . Turn your prayer book to page five."

I'm going to have a great eulogy. I just added to my list of things I must take care of before I go—get a good eulogist. Someone who's going to tell it like it is. Sheila Levine died for your sins.

Harold

THEY SAY that when two people are trying to have a baby and the woman can't conceive, it may be because they're trying too hard. The obstetrician suggests they relax. Usually this doesn't work. The couple adopts, and immediately after, the little woman gets pregnant.

I was trying too hard to catch a man, and I should have relaxed, but I couldn't. I went out and bought a plot and tombstone, and shortly afterward I met someone. Don't get excited—I didn't say I got married or engaged or anything. I merely said I met a man.

I went to this election eve party. It wasn't even a national or mayoral election, which will show you to what length New Yorkers will go in order to congregate. I still went to parties. Not because I was looking for a man, but because if I stopped going to parties, people might become suspicious of my actions.

"What's with Sheila? She used to go to every party she was invited to. Now she's staying home. There must be something wrong."

So I was at this party given by one of the girls I taught with, just sitting there eating a huge sandwich and potato salad because I really didn't care anymore. This dark, stocky guy with a lot of hair, not bad-looking, not good-looking, came up to me and sat down just as I was putting a rather large pickle into my mouth.

"Hi." (He said that)

"Hi." (Me)

"I hate to beat around the bush. I'd like to fuck you." (Him . . . did you think it was me?)

"I hate to beat around the bush, too. How many minutes do you think it will take?" I hate myself when I'm flip. Why can't I be Doris Day?

(Him again) "I said I'd like to sleep with you."

(Me) "I said for how many minutes?"

(Him) "That's not a very nice question."

(Me) "Yours was nice?"

I slept with/fucked with Harold that very night. Yes, I managed to find out his name and a few other details of his life. He was thirty-three, divorced, Jewish, maybe-marriageable and a social worker-poet.

On this election eve I couldn't believe my good fortune. Harold was bright, had a good, friendly personality, and I had an orgasm. Yes, folks, this time I knew it. I was sure. Let me tell you—when you have it, you know it.

Mom, I know you're asking why. Why would a nice Jewish girl hop into the sack just because some guy asks her to? I feel you are entitled to an explanation. And if I can help one other Jewish girl who reads this stay out of some slob's bed, then I shall not have died in vain.

I am not oversexed. My tits did not titillate. If you'd rather read about titillating tits, go read *Cosmo*. When I was in college, I slept with guys because it made me feel popular. When I moved into New York, I went to bed with guys because I thought in my marriage-centered brain that if I went to bed with them, they might like me. If one of them really liked me, he might, oh, please, dear God, marry me. I went to bed with them all thinking that maybe my mama would dance at my wedding. I went to bed with Harold because I was used to going to bed with men when they asked me to.

"Manny, look, see how they blame everything on the mother."

Don't feel bad, Mom. Orgasms are good.

Harold stayed all night. It was nice. So nice to wake up and see him there, to give him towels and toast, to squeeze an orange, to make love again in the morning, in the afternoon, in the early evening. Three more orgasms, folks. He left after dinner . . . I was dinner.

I didn't think I would ever hear from him again. Miracle of miracles, Harold called the following Saturday.

"Hi."

"Hi."

"It's Harold. I'd like to fuck you tonight."

"You certainly get right to the point."

"Well?"

"Come over. We'll talk."

"We'll talk, hell. That night I had my fifth climax. Have you had five orgasms, Mom? Ruthie? Madeline? Melissa? I'll bet you've had five all together. Not that many, you say?

Harold slept over again. We spent Sunday making love and talking about how great the sexual revolution was. To tell you the truth, the sexual revolution was making me sore, if you know what I mean. This time when Harold left, he looked straight into my close-set brown eyes with the untweezed eyebrows and said, "I'd like to fuck you next Wednesday."

I avoided his beady little eyes, which sat on top of his overgrown beard, and said, "Great."

"I'm happy I found you, Sheila. You are truly a liberated woman." (You hear that, Mom? A liberated woman!)

"Yeah."

So I thought, what's so bad? Could be worse. I'd have three dirty, hippie children, radical chic, and three hundred and sixty-five orgasms a year.

On Tuesday night I got my period. Always a celebration at my house. I called Harold at work the next day to tell him he'd better not come over.

"Hello, is Harold there? I'm sorry I don't know his last name. He's short, stocky, has a beard." (He sleeps with Sheila Levine.)

"Hello, Harold? I'm sorry, you can't come over tonight. I just got my period."

"This isn't Harold. It's Jerry. You want Harold?" (Oh, God!)

"Yes . . . please." (It's not the type of message you leave on someone's desk.)

"Hello."

"Hello, Harold?" (I was going to be sure this time.)

"Yes, Sheila?"

"Yes, listen, Harold. You can't come over tonight. I have my period."

"I know. Jerry told me."

"I just wanted you to know."

"I don't care if you're hemorrhaging. I'm coming."

He came, too. Several times. Harold had decided he wanted me on Wednesday night, and he got me. Three hundred and sixty-five climaxes a year was an accurate figure.

Our relationship went on like this for a month. About three weeks after I met Harold, I was thinking so maybe it had happened at last. Harold wasn't proposing, but maybe I could get him to live with me for seven years and I could become his common-law wife. (How do you celebrate anniversaries? When does he give you the cocktail ring with the diamond baguettes?)

On the fourth Saturday, après sex, Harold got dressed, went to the door and said, "You've been great."

"I've been great?"

"Yeah. I'd like to fuck you Christmas Eve."

He left. He also left me with a fungus. The kind of

176

fungus you're embarrassed to go to your gynecologist with. I would have forgotten about Harold much sooner if it wasn't for that goddamned itch.

So guess who called a few weeks later? Harold the itch, Harold the bitch, the fungus. I was hoping he'd call. I wanted to tell him off.

"Hello, Sheila."

"Yes."

"Is this the Sheila with the big boobs?"

"Yes, I mean no, yes, who is this?"

"It's Harold. Remember? We met at an election eve party. We fucked a few times."

"Oh, yes."

"I was wondering if it's still on for Christmas Eve."

"What?" (I was playing hard to get to bed. Isn't that cute?)

"We were gonna fuck Christmas Eve, remember?"

"Well, Harold, I don't know. You haven't called, I'm still scratching."

"What?"

"Nothing."

"Listen, Sheila, in addition to Christmas Eve, I was wondering if you'd be free New Year's Eve." (New Year's Eve? I had latched onto some guy with a holiday fetish.)

"I don't know." (New Year's Eve. My last New Year's on earth. Was I going to spend it with Harold? Would he give me another fungus—ring out the old fungus—bring in the new.)

"Come on, Sheila baby."

"Okay."

"Great, baby, see you Christmas Eve. Keep the peace."

So I have a date for New Year's Eve. I like the idea. Know what I'm gonna do? I'm going to take my li'l ol' charge card and buy me a beautiful party dress and wear it on New Year's Eve—even if we don't go out.

I need something to be buried in anyway. Can I find the perfect dress for both occasions?

"May I help you?"

"Yes, you may. I'm looking for a dress for New Year's Eve."

"Right this way."

"Do you happen to have something that will be good for New Year's Eve and appropriate for a funeral in July?"

"Why, I don't know. That all depends what you're planning to do New Year's Eve."

"Screw."

"Pardon me."

"I said, screw. I'm planning to screw on New Year's Eve."

"We have several dresses that would be suitable for that. May I ask who the gentleman is—perhaps that will help me narrow it down."

"Certainly. His name is Harold."

"Harold! You're kidding! Tell that fucking son of a bitch when you see him that he gave me a fungus."

Harold did, as planned, come over Christmas Eve. This time he brought me more than an itch. He had wrapped in tissue one small daisy, which is—you must admit—hard to find around Christmas in New York. It really was quite touching, and so was Harold.

My sixth orgasm—all with Harold, and I was feeling very close to him. The daisy really got to me. He was obviously going to spend the night, and he had, I am sure, more than visions of sugar plums floating in his head. The moment was right. I decided to tell Harold about my suicide. Why? Did I expect him to beg me not to do it? Was I hoping for some sign of love? Was I trying to shock him? I don't know why. There was no one else to tell. I couldn't tell my parents, my sister, my students. Maybe it was the fungus. He had given me something to worry about, and I was going to return the favor.

"Harold?"

"You had another orgasm, didn't you?"

"Yes."

"I'm pretty good, aren't I?"

"Yes, pretty good."

"Whadda you mean, pretty good. I'm damned good. I'm absolutely the best fucker in the world." (The mood was great. We were smiling and talking at the same time.)

"Harold?"

"What?"

"I'm going to kill myself."

"What?" (Not a shocking "what." Just a questioning "what.")

"I'm going to kill myself. I'm going to commit suicide."

"Really?"

"Yeah, really. I've been thinking about it for a long time now. I'm really going to do it." (Say something. Say something to make me change my mind. Marry me.)

"Like wow! That really blows my mind. I'm fucking a girl who's going to commit suicide. When? Have you decided?"

"July third. I'm going to do it July third so that the funeral can be July fourth."

"Wow, that's really something. You really are some great chick. Wow! You're really going to commit suicide. Boy, does that turn me on!" (He lunged for my body.) Seven orgasms.

Harold had breakfast and early-morning sex with me the next day.

"Sheila?"

"Yes."

"Is there anything I can do to help?"

"Nah. I'll clean it up myself."

"No, I mean about the suicide. Is there anything I can do to help?"

"What do you mean, help?"

"I'd like to help in some way. Like help you get the pills or something. I have some good connections when it comes to pills."

"I'll let you know if I need you. Thanks."

"I'd really like to help in some way. I'd feel terrible if I didn't help in some way." (There was a man with a conscience.)

"I'm sure there's something you could do. You could send daisies for the casket. That would be lovely."

"Wow! I'll do that. I'll send daisies. You just tell me where and I'll send them."

"Thanks, Harold."

That afternoon. . . .

"Sheila?"

"Yes?"

"I know it's a personal question and we don't know each other that well [no, we've just touched each other's privates a lot], but I would like to know why you're doing it."

"I'm doing it because I like sex." (Yeah, Mom, what the hell. A few more orgasms before I go. Just a few more aren't going to kill me.)

"No, I don't mean why you are doing that. I mean why are you going to kill yourself?"

"It's a long story. I'm writing a long suicide note. You can read it if you want to."

"Where is it?"

"Not now. You can read it when I'm dead."

"Wow! Come here, you!" Nine orgasms all in a row.

"Sheila?"

"Yes?"

"I bet you don't go through with it."

"With the suicide?"

"Yeah."

"Look!" (I leaned out of bed and got the DECEASED stamp from my desk drawer. I took it out of the paper and showed it to Harold.)

"Wow!"

Harold came by, off and on, the days between Christmas and New Year's. He treated me as if I were going to die—but not by my own hand—as if I were very sick and the doctor told me I had only six months to live. He brought me little presents, funny earmuffs and a bottle of cheap champagne. Now I *have* to die. I mean, it would be pretty embarrassing after the earmuffs and the champagne and his being so nice for me to change my mind. Funny . . . Harold gave me the responsibility to die. He's turned into a very nice, understanding lover, who is doing everything possible to make my last moments on earth happy ones. The responsibility is overwhelming. When somebody is being so nice and buys you presents, you can't very well turn around, and change your mind, can you? Death is a very complex thing.

"Sheila?"

"Yeah?"

"It's a gas."

"What's a gas, Harold?"

"What you're going to do."

"You mean killing myself?"

"Yeah. It's a gas. There are not many girls like you. You've really got guts."

"Yeah."

"Come 'ere, you." (And I went there and I went there and I went there.)

The honest-to-God truth of the matter is that I have finally turned a guy on and the only way to keep him turned on is to bury myself within the year.

New Year's Eve was great. Really fantastic. Naturally, I always hated New Year's Eve. Either I had no date and spent the night with a girlfriend who slept over after watching the ball fall on television or I had a date with a guy who just needed a date to take to some crummy party and he asked me rather than sit home himself. Or . . . I had a blind date. Terrible, right? A blind date on New Year's Eve means locking yourself in the ladies' room at twelve o'clock so that you won't have to kiss him when the lights go out. Melissa, of course, always had a date for New Year's Eve around Thanksgiving. Some poor Corvette owner once called only three weeks in advance. Miss Melissa hung up in his face. Are you surprised that New Year's Eves were pure torture for yours truly? No, you're not surprised. You expected that from old Sheila.

This year was different. Harold came to the door at about eight, wearing a very nice new suit. That may not seem very important to you, but to me it was a miracle. A new suit was not something I had seen often. Really, men just never did wear new suits for me. Harold's was brown, no—tan, wide lapels and great.

"I like your suit."

"It's new."

I was wearing a long skirt and blouse, very festive, half from Ohrbach's, half from Saks.

"I like your dress."

"It's a blouse and a skirt."

"It's great."

"I was thinking of getting buried in it."

"No."

"Whadda you mean 'no'?" (No? What do you mean? No, don't die?)

"You should be buried nude and have an open casket."

"You're kidding."

"No, I'm not, Sheila. You don't think you have a

great body, but it happens to turn me on. I'll bet it would turn on all the guys in the funeral parlor, like it turns me on." (So, before we went out, we did it. Is it a crime?)

"Sheila, since this is your last New Year's on earth, it's going to be the best." And it was—most of it was.

We turned on and went to Times Square. (No, this was not the first time for me. I am a sophisticated woman of the world, who has smoked grass and hash at least a dozen times. The first time was on Fire Island.)

People. A hundred, million, billion people. God, they were ugly. They didn't go to dentists, those people. There was a lot of noise and a lot of smell. Harold held onto me tightly, pushing my long-line bra into my ribs. You have to do it once. I hated it down there, but I'm glad I did it once. It somehow made me feel pretty. Yeah, I was the girl in Times Square with the prettiest teeth. We didn't stay till twelve, just whisked in, said our hellos, and whisked right out again. A fuzzy experience.

Harold was invited to two parties—the one he had to go to and the one he wanted to go to. Naturally, we got the "had to go" out of the way quickly. It was given by Harold's cousin, Marty Feinberg, same last name as Harold's. It was in an old, ill-furnished West End Avenue apartment, a few widowed aunts and—surprise!—Harold's former wife.

"Hello, Harold."

"Hello, Frannie, how are you?"

"A lot you care."

"What makes you think I don't care?"

"The kids came back dirty last weekend."

"They had a great time. I'm sure they had more fun with their dirty father than they do all week with their sterile mother."

"The same old Harold."

"The same old Frannie."

"Very cute, Harold. One of these days, I'm going to slap you into alimony jail."

"I'm paying."

"You're paying child support. What about me? What do you expect me to do on fifty-two fifty a week? I had to take a part-time job while the kids are in school."

"Aw, poor Frannie has to work."

"You'll see, you'll see all too soon, Harold. One of these days, you'll wake up with a subpoena in your face."

"Nice to talk to you again, Frannie. You reconfirmed my faith in divorce."

"Go to hell."

"Go fuck yourself—no one else will."

A lot of people have said to me that I shouldn't worry about getting married—that soon there will be a whole new crop of divorced men. I don't want to be the second wife. I want to be the first wife—the one he leaves because she doesn't clean and charges up a storm.

We left cousin Marty's party at about eleven thirty and tried to race to Marsha and David's, another one of your nice young couples who are living together because he feels marriage has had it. Harold is friendly with David from the Welfare Department and I knew Marsha slightly at NYU.

What's the worst thing that can happen to you when the clock strikes twelve, New Year's Eve? The worst thing is being alone. The second worst thing is being in the subway. Nobody notices that the New Year is in. Some couples kiss, but they've been kissing from the moment they boarded. Some are alone. The smell of vomit is in the air. The worst off are those who are, at twelve midnight, going home from jobs. They're the members of society who have no choice . . . the ones

184

who work New Year's Eve or lose their jobs. God, it's sad.

At twelve Harold simply took my hand. The gesture made kissing seem trite.

Marsha and David's. Marsha and David lived on West Fifty-seventh between Sixth and Seventh in a three-room apartment, separate bedroom. The minute you walked in the door, you could tell Marsha and David were not married.

There were two hi-fi's in the living room. There was a lot of his and her food, like imported beer and organic vegetable juice. Married couples have common food, like Seven-Up, maybe a little apple cider. Marsha had service for eight—four of one pattern, four of another.

In the bedroom, where we put our coats, two checkbooks from different banks. Unmarried. And in the bathroom, only one robe—his—and no monogrammed towels. And on the front door, only his name.

Marsha served chili and the music was slow and the company divine and we couldn't wait to get home to bed. We got our coats and sneaked out without saying good-bye. We taxied home and were undressed by the time we reached my front door. Another you-know-what and I've lost count.

"Harold?"

"Yeah?"

"Marsha and David seem happy, don't they?"

"Sheila, don't."

"Don't what?"

"Ask me to live with you."

He left the next morning. A week went by, and I didn't hear from him. I didn't call him. I was tempted, but I didn't call. That was my training. "Sheila, darling, boys don't like to be chased." Another week. I couldn't stand it. I picked up the phone, dialed his number and

185

hung up—several times. By the third week I was calling regularly. Every day. No—every ten minutes—until two, three in the morning. He was never in, and I could only assume he was living with someone. I was very glad I hadn't canceled the plot.

February 4

Dear Sheila,

I guess you're wondering why I haven't called you or anything. Maybe you're not wondering. [I'm wondering, I'm wondering. It's been over a month, and I have no idea where my next orgasm is coming from. Don't be selfish, Sheila, there are people in India who go to sleep without orgasms.] In any case, I thought I'd write and tell you what's happened.

Remember when we went to my cousin's party on New Year's Eve? [Yeah!] Remember my ex-wife was there? [Yeah.] Do you remember when she threatened to send me to alimony jail? [Yeah, I do . . . don't tell me that. . . .] Well, the bitch did it. Slapped me into alimony jail.

I got the subpoena about four weeks ago, and my lawyer tried to get me out of it, but, Sheila, I refused to pay the dough. I'd rather sit here a million years and rot—I'm in for six months—than give that bitch one penny. For the kids—yes. For the bitch—no.

It's not too bad in here. You wouldn't believe it, a whole jail full of guys who didn't pay alimony. Executives, teachers, all kinds. One millionaire, the guys say.

Sheila, you're the only one I've written to. I want you to do me a big favor. PLEASE! I want you to buy some pot and mail it to me—in something—like the inside of a book or something. You think of a way. You're a very clever girl.

Love,
HAROLD

OH, BOY! Sheila Levine gets caught and is slapped in jail herself for buying, possessing and sending marijuana through the U.S. mail. I've never sent even a dirty word through the mails. My big worry was that I'd be caught and be in jail, or doing hard labor, on July 3.

First I read and reread the letter. He said, "Love, Harold." Does that mean "love," or is it just a way of signing off? He also said that he will be in jail for six months, and six months from when he went in is the end of July. I'll be all gone by the time he gets out. No more Sheila. There's only five months left, and I had counted on Harold for at least five lays. I had a right to those lays.

I flushed his letter down the toilet—there shouldn't be evidence.

How do you find pot? It just always seemed to be around. I called all the pot smokers I knew and spoke to them in hushed tones over the telephone. The town was "dry." Everyone would let me know if they located any. Oh, God, Harold, why didn't you ask for a file in a cake, like all the other prisoners?

What do I do now? Do I meet some dirty little man in Needle Park or Columbus Circle? . . . "You'll know me. I'm five five, a little chubby, have wavy hair, and I'll be wearing my real nose. How will I know you?" . . . "I'll be wearing an old jacket, old pants, and I'll look like I need a fix. I'll also be carrying a knife to slit your throat in case I don't like your looks."

February 7

Dear Harold,

I was very sorry to hear what happened to you, but it will all be over soon. [I write terrible letters.] I don't know where to buy the delicious "cookies" you wanted. I guess I've gone to "pot" without you. Please tell me where I can find the "cookies" and how I go about buying them.

Nothing much is new, except I bought some new "pots" and pans and can't wait to cook with them. Hope to hear from you soon.

Love ya,
SHEILA

187

P.S. I have quite a bit of money saved up, and if you need it, I'll be happy to give it to you for your back alimony payments. After all, you can't take it with you. Ha! Ha! [The dying woman jests.]

S. L.

P.P.S. Really, the money is yours if you want it.

S.

I thought "love ya" was much better than "love" because "love" is used by everyone. A very subtle difference, but I felt the "love ya" was stronger in this case.

February 12

Dear Sheila,
    You can call a girl named Marcia Phillips, 555-8965. She'll get you the "cookies." She'll also get you some great marijuana—a lid for about twenty bucks. Let me know exactly how much and I'll pay you back.
    Thank you very much for your lovely offer of your life savings. No, thank you. I don't want the bitch to have your money, Sheila. I think I can last the six months.

Love ya,
HAROLD

He can last the six months, but I can't. Somehow I'm gonna get him out of there. I can face dying, but I'm not going to masturbate my way to the grave. "Love ya, Harold" indeed. I flushed it down the toilet, but cut the "love ya" off and put it on my mirror.
    555-8965, sixteen rings and no answer. I tried every day for a week. 555-8965, sixteen rings and no answer.

February 21

Dear Harold,
    The "cookie" lady is not in. I tried several times, but she never answers. Do you think she got picked up for selling "cookies" or something?

My love,
SHEILA

Dear Sheila,

If Marcia has been picked up, it would be the first time in the history of New York that someone was busted for selling cookies. Listen, Sheila, ask around. Ask a few hip people. Everyone in New York knows where to get pot. [Another letter down the toilet.] I know you can do it, Sheila baby.

My love,
HAROLD

OH, BOY! "Excuse me, miss" . . . "Could I help you? Would you like to see something in an evening dress?" . . . "No, I was wondering if you know where I can find some pot." SIRENS, store detectives everywhere.

"Paper! Get your paper! Paper, miss?" . . . "No, but I'd like some pot." POLICE WHISTLE, into the paddy wagon.

JOSHUA! Joshua would know. He was the first pot smoker I ever met. So where's Joshua? Last I heard, he was selling diaper service to expectant young mothers. Those diaper companies used a lot of actors out of work. . . . "Hello, Tidy-Didy, do you have a Joshua working for you?" . . . "No." . . . "Happy-Dri, do you have a Joshua working for you?" . . . "No."

I put an ad in the *Village Voice:* Joshua, Sheila Levine wants you to call, KL5-4394. Joshua didn't call, but Ronald Fell, a friend of Joshua's, called and wanted to know if I heard from Joshua. He left me his number in case I heard anything.

The light bulb over my head.

"Hi, Ronald, this is Sheila Levine. I have something to ask you. You're going to think I'm crazy, but [Careful now, Sheila, the wires are probably tapped. The FBI is on your phone] what I'd like to know, if you know, and you probably don't know—a nice boy like you. I'd like to know where I can find some . . . [in a whisper] some pot."

189

"What?" (Ronald, you idiot! Don't you realize we're being listened to and followed?)

"Do you know where I can find some pot?" (Whispering again.)

"What? Sheila, I can't hear you." (Ronald, I'm sorry. I didn't know you'd get into trouble, too. I thought they'd just send *me* to jail because I did the asking.)

"Do you know where I can get some pot?" (Coming in nice and clear in some officer's ear.)

"Why don't you call Shelly Krupp or Luke or Marcia Phillips or, listen, I'm picking some up on Thursday night? Do you want a lid?"

"Yes, please."

"You sound like you need some pretty bad."

"Yeah, Ronald, I really do."

"I'll pick it up Thursday night. Why don't you come down here about eleven. I'm at . . . you got a pencil?"

"Yeah, go ahead."

"I'm at 412 East Sixth, apartment Four C."

"Do you want the money in advance or anything?"

"Nah. See you then."

"Thanks, Ronald."

"Nothing."

I took a cab to East Sixth, got the stuff, took a cab back home, was sure the taxi driver was an undercover agent, was sure the doorman spotted my package and called the police. I had the "stuff" in my underwear drawer . . . NO! It's not safe there. In the bathroom . . . NO! That's the first place they'd look. In a box, in a suitcase in a closet, buried under boxes of shoes.

I mailed it off to Harold inside a Snoopy doll that I scooped out. What they thought a grown man was doing with a Snoopy doll was Harold's problem.

March 17

Dear Sheila,
Thanks for the Snoopy with the big "pot." Every

kid should get one for Christmas. I wish I could give you a great big kiss. [So do I.]

Love,
HAROLD

So he was back to "Love." I'm going to get him out of there if it's the last thing I do.

March 27

Dear Harold,

I am fine and hope you are the same. [Brilliant opening] Not much is new. [Great letter] What's new with you? [Such a way with words!]

Harold, do you remember when I offered to pay your back alimony so that you could get out of jail? Well, I really meant it. I have some money in the bank, and I really don't need it. I have to pay the balance on the tombstone. I have to buy a dress to be buried in and a casket. I have to pay a lawyer to draw up the will, and I have to buy some new underwear for when they find me dead in the apartment. [They shouldn't find me in old underwear. How would it look?] Besides that, I have nothing to do with my money. Harold, you can have it. Really. Hoping this letter is finding you well. [Strong finish]

Love,
SHEILA

Monday, Tuesday, Wednesday, Thursday—no answer. On Friday, the phone rang, and it was Harold. I never knew that prisoners could make phone calls.

"Hello, Sheila?"

"Harold, where are you?"

"Just where I've been for the last few months—safe and sound on the inside."

"They let you make calls?"

"Yeah, maybe they'll let me make love. Wanna come and visit?"

"I thought only wives were allowed to visit."

"Darling, this is alimony jail. Nobody here is interested in visiting wives."

"Harold, what I really want is for you to come out. You can have my money. I have over two thousand dollars. You can have it, Harold."

"No, I can't have it. If you give it to me, I have to give it to Frannie, who slept late and pretended to have headaches when it was time to screw. I don't want her to have it."

"I want her to have it, Harold. I want her to have it so that I can have you."

"Oh, Sheila, do you know what I wish and I'm not even high? I wish I had met you before Frannie fucked me up for life. She did, Sheila. I am no longer capable of giving love or receiving love. Frannie did that to me."

"Maybe if I. . . ."

"No, Sheila."

Why? Why is my last involvement on earth a pile of shit?

The End

So, Harold, come on out already. Sheila needs you. The months of her life are moving quickly by and you won't budge. It's the merry month of May, Harold. Come out, come out wherever you are.

May 6

Dear Harold,

Harold, I need you. Not for very long. I need you for now. Your being in prison forces me to be in prison. Less than two months, Harold, that's all I have. It's too late to find someone new.

I promise you, Harold, I won't make demands. You can see me or not see me. Live here or not live here. Just come on out, Harold. I have the money. The plot is paid for. The tombstone is paid for. How much could a plain casket, a will and some new underwear cost?

Please, Harold. Come on out.

Love,
SHEILA

So why was I begging? Was there still life in me? Had I not given up yet? Was I expecting Harold to change my life, to force the poison from my mouth and make me live? Did I just want a few good lays, or did I want someone to stop me from doing what I planned to do last August? Was I planning a phony suicide? The kind where I'd call someone at the last minute to save me? I think so and I don't think so and

I don't really know. I went forward with my plans. I still expected to go in July . . . unless. Unless what? Unless nothing, Sheila. Stop being so fucking dramatic.

Dear Sheila,

You win. I'm tired of sitting here with nothing but paperbacks and pot. It'll cost you $2,300. I'm sorry, Sheila, that's what the bitch is demanding. You don't know how low I feel taking it from you and giving it to her. I feel low and obligated.

HAROLD

No "Love, Harold." Just "Harold."

"Sheila?"

"Harold, where are you?"

"I'm out. I'm standing here on the corner of Twenty-ninth and Tenth in a telephone booth."

"Come on over, Harold. You can stay here if you want."

"I'll be over soon. Got to pick up some stuff. See you."

He sounded so down. I made a mistake. I didn't need Harold. What I needed was a casket.

Harold sat there on my black corduroy bedspread with the black and white throw pillows just watching me night and day. He was stoned all the time—probably because he resented me for buying his way out of jail. And things in bed just weren't what they used to be. In the first three weeks, we had sex about seven times and out of those seven, I only had three orgasms. Twenty-three hundred dollars is a lot to pay for three orgasms.

He left the apartment sometimes for hours, sometimes for days. He returned at odd hours, eating chocolate, smoking, sniffing, snorting and looking skinny. And all the time he talked about going to Canada. It was scary. He sat there on my bedspread just waiting for me to go—like a vulture. Now he feels obligated. When I'm gone, he'll feel he did the best he could. You know what I did? I bought a lot of aggravation.

"I wish I had your guts, Sheila. I wish I had the guts to kill myself."

"What guts? It doesn't take guts. It takes exhaustion. I'm just too tired to live."

And he lit up another joint, and he still sat on my spread, but he was gone for the night. The dope wasn't my scene, and Harold wasn't my scene anymore either. How the hell, fuck, bitch, was I going to be found on my bed if he wouldn't remove himself from the premises?

I couldn't help him— Like, Harold, don't you think you've had enough drugs?— The nagging wife.

I couldn't ask him to go. I asked him to come.

So I gotta find a hip rabbi. I told you the eulogy my poor Great-Aunt Goldie Butkin had. I did not want light words spoken over my dead body. (My body is pretty dead. Harold is here, but I'm telling you the dope went straight to his penis. It ain't what it used to be.)

Go find a hip rabbi. I gotta have a rabbi, right? Face it. If I don't find one, Mr. and Mrs. Levine will. They'll get the old, friendly neighborhood rabbi, who will tell everyone gathered there to grieve about what a nice girl I was and how I went to Sunday school. Is that what I want to leave the folks with? It is not. I want a rabbi who's going to tell it like it is. (Was?)

SHEILA LEVINE KILLED HERSELF BECAUSE THERE WEREN'T ENOUGH MEN TO GO AROUND. SHE DIDN'T HAVE BAD BREATH. SHE USED VAGINAL SPRAY. SHE TRIED FOR TEN YEARS. BUT SHE DIDN'T MAKE IT. NO ONE EVER WANTED HER FOR FOREVER. SHEILA LEVINE DIED FOR OUR SINS.

Where am I gonna find a rabbi to express my sentiments? A recent graduate from a rabbinical college? Someone from the Village? Yeah. Remember that temple that used to always wish their Christian neighbors a happy easter, or whatever it is you wish on Easter.

"Hello, is this the temple?"

"Yes."

"Hello. My name is Sheila Levine. [Get the name in quickly, she shouldn't think some non-Jewish person is calling.] I would like to talk to the rabbi, if I may."

"Who wouldn't? Rabbi Stine is in—he's out. He's running all around. We never see him. He never sits down. Not for a minute. I'll be happy to leave your name for him, but I have no idea when he'll call. Wait, I'll get a pencil and I'll get your name, and may I ask what is the nature of the business you have with the rabbi?"

"Sheila Levine and my number is Lebines."

"What?"

"Lebines. You dial L-E-B-I-N-E-S. My telephone number happens to be my name—almost." I thought that was pretty clever. A friend of mine's number was DARLING.

"Let me write that down." She sounded very cold, too cold to be working for a rabbi.

"And the nature of the business you wish to speak to the rabbi about?"

"It's personal . . . about a eulogy."

"I only ask because he's so busy and if I can help him out in any way, I do. Richard, take that to the front office."

So now I sit and wait for the busy Rabbi Stine to call. I didn't actually sit and wait. I sort of lay down and waited with Harold on top of me. Nothing. The going rate is still twenty-three hundred dollars for three orgasms—get 'em while they're hot.

Three days went by, and I called Rabbi Stine again. He was there. Actually in his office. I had to hold for twenty minutes.

"Hello." (I knew it was Rabbi Stine. His voice was rushed. I talked at a brisk pace. I didn't want to take up one minute more of the rabbi's time than I had to, and isn't that the way it always is with rabbis?)

"Hello, my name is Sheila Levine. I would like to make an appointment with you about a eulogy . . . my eulogy. What time is convenient for you?" (I expected compassion. I expected tears in his voice as he told me that he would visit my home and there we could talk things out.)

"I'll put my secretary on. She'll make an appointment." (Click. He accidentally disconnected me, this servant of the Lord.)

"Hello, my name is Sheila Levine. I was just talking to Rabbi Stine and he asked me to hold and make an appointment with his secretary, but we were cut off."

"Thursday at six and please be here exactly at six. The rabbi has a class at six thirty. I don't know how he does it."

"Thank you."

Let me tell you about Rabbi Stine. Gorgeous. Not in your glossy Rock Hudson way. A young Paul Newman. Blue eyes you could die from. Long blondish hair underneath a yarmulke. He made men look foolish for not wearing one. You know the young Israeli look? That's Rabbi Stine. No wedding band, and I asked myself—what am I so excited about? I'm not going out with him. He's going to be officiating at my funeral, where my heart will no longer be able to go thumpity-thump. Forget him, Sheila. He's six feet tall, and you'll be six feet under.

We faced each other. The two of us alone in a temple. One of us had dirty thoughts.

"Rabbi, I recently went to a funeral . . . that's not important. Rabbi, I would like you to hear me out before you say anything."

"I'm listening." (He's listening like Paul Newman would be listening. Rabbi Stine is arrogant and gorgeous. Is that a combination?)

"Rabbi, I have planned to kill myself on July third and will be buried July fourth. I am killing myself because I wanted to get married and my mother wanted me to get married and I never did get married, and I'm tired of the embarrassment of it all. I would like you to officiate at the funeral because if you don't, some strange rabbi will say a lot of prayers that would be meaningless to me and no one in the whole memorial chapel at Rossman's Memorial Park will know why I died. I want them to know why I died. I want them to know. It's important to me."

"Sheila, you sound very determined. Can't I in some way prevent this?"

"Only by marrying me." (I turned away, for I was feeling tears.)

"I'm going to do it!"

"What?" (Marry me!!?)

"I'm going to tell them why you died, Sheila. Everyone at Rossman's Memorial Park will know why Sheila Levine killed herself."

"Great."

"Harold, Rabbi Stine is going to do the eulogy."

"Heavy," he said in a very down tone.

"Harold, you know you don't have to stay here if you don't want to. I mean, I don't want you to stay if you don't want to."

"Don't you want me to stay?"

"Sure, I want you to stay if you want to stay, but I don't want you to feel you *have* to stay."

"I'm staying because I want to stay." (And he cried.)

"Harold? Harold? What's the matter? Come on, Harold, what's the matter?"

"Nothing's the matter. Sheila, I want you to do me a favor."

"Sure, Harold."

"I want you to go down to the East Village and get me some coke. I'd go, but I'm sick. Really, Sheila."

"Oh, Christ, Harold. I just found out about getting pot, now you want me to get coke. Harold, I would . . . only . . . Harold, for God's sake, can't you call them and have them deliver or something?"

"You dumb middle-class broad. You don't call and have coke delivered. You go down to the slums and you buy it. Right down to the slums."

"And you want me to go 'down to the slums' and risk my life getting you coke?"

"Risk your life? Oh, Sheila. Risk your life? You're killing yourself. What do you mean risk your life?"

"Okay, okay, Harold, I'll go. Why don't I go now and buy with my own hands a whole lot of poison for you to take? Don't you realize, Harold, you're killing yourself?"

"So are you."

SLAM.

Down to the East Village and follow the directions. The nicest thing about knowing you're going to die soon is taking cabs. Spend it while you can. You never know what's going to happen. You could slip in the shower. Get hit by a car. Accidentally slash your wrists. We passed Washington Square Park, and it reconfirmed my faith in suicide. I love the park. There's just no goddamn place for me to sit in it. The college kids are around the fountain. The junkies are by the statue. The old men are by the game tables, and the young mothers are with their kids near the swings and seesaws. No section for a single girl to rest her weary bones.

Up some crummy stairs, into some crummy apartment. Harold sent me. I've come for the stuff. Trite as it may seem, it was the East Village hippie scene that's in all the movies. Mattresses on the floor and a skinny, soft-spoken girl. Two guys smoking pot. Just like in the movies. Wow! A block from where Sheila and Linda wanted to rent—a century ago.

I paid for the coke like I was buying candy in a candy store.

"Er, excuse me? Could you tell me what's the best thing for me to take to kill myself? Like, is there one pill that would really do it quickly and with no pain, if you know what I mean?"

"What do you wanna do that for?"

"It's a long story. I just wanted to know if you knew of anything. Never mind. Good-bye and thanks. Harold sends his love and peace." (He hadn't sent that, but I figured that was the appropriate thing to say.)

"Peace."

You know what I realized that day? I'm very, very old.

All of a sudden Harold cheered up. I think it was because he saw the end approaching. Only a month and a half to go. What a blessing for Harold. How chipper he was feeling. Not that Harold didn't care for me. It's just that I was an albatross around his neck. Now, if you had an albatross around your neck and you knew that albatross was going to commit suicide in about a month and a half, you'd cheer up too. Right? Sure, right. So when have I been wrong?

Harold was taking fewer pills, smoking less pot, sniffing less coke. He was, you might say, high on my suicide. He even went with me to buy the dress (decided not to wear the New Year's Eve number—too hot for a summer funeral) and wig that I was to be buried in (Yes. A wig. I always wanted long, straight, blond hair and I was going to have it in that box. Which reminds me—I've got to buy the box, too. Shit! I forgot about that.)

I needed a dress, I needed a wig, and I needed great underwear. And money was no object. Well, it was a little bit of an object—like I wasn't going for a two-thousand-dollar Balenciaga, but I was willing to go over a hundred. After all, it's not every day a girl gets buried. And, when you think about it, I really would be getting a lot of wear out of that one dress. If I were going to be frozen, I would definitely go for more. That can be a problem. Suppose you're frozen in a fantastic dress and it's out of style by the time you're defrosted!

First we went to Ohrbach's—but aha—not to the departments that the career girls and yentas go to. To the Grey Room, where Anne Ford goes. (Read about her every year at the Ohrbach's fashion show.) That's where they have the line-by-line copy of all the originals, same material and everything. We looked at a few dresses, a Valentino copy, a Dior copy. I tried on a couple and found out, this late in life, that to wear a line-by-line copy, you need a line-by-line copy of the body that Anne Ford has.

I sort of liked one, but I didn't like the way I looked in it lying down. (Yes, the salesgirl caught me lying down, but I said I was looking for an earring.) I figured it's the last dress I'm ever gonna buy, so why settle? I mean, lying down is how I'm gonna be, even though the plot is on a hill.

Out of Ohrbach's and up to Lord & Taylor's. The second floor.

"May I help you?" (You can always tell when those charming salesl023ies are working on commission. This one practically grabbed me right off the elevator.)

"I'm looking for something semidressy, semilong, semi. . . ."

"She's looking for something to be buried in." (Harold, cheerfully)

201

"Right this way, please." (Yep, for sure. She was working on commission.)

As we were walking right this way, we passed, on a mannequin, a fantastic gypsyish dress. I loved it, wanted it for my very own. Money is no object, and it'd better not be too expensive.

"Excuse me, miss, do you think that maybe there's a slight chance somehow that they might have this dress in my size, a thirteen, if it runs large."

"I'll check." (Did she not hear what Harold said about me being buried in it or did she not care? Just get the sale. Ring up the ol' commission. If she heard and didn't care, I might as well tell Henry Rossman that the small chapel for memorial services would do just fine. Something tells me that there isn't going to be a fantastic turnout.)

She checked and we browsed, Harold just a-whistling and a-humming and getting ready to dance on my grave. (I should have been cremated and made him dance on my urn.) I spotted a few other dresses that would do nicely, but nothing as nice as the gypsy-lady one.

She had it in size thirteen, led me to a dressing room and let me know in no uncertain terms that she was Mrs. Landman, my salesgirl, if I needed help to let her know, the name is Landman. Put me in the dressing room and put her name, "Landman," in a little plastic slot right outside the door. That's to let the other salesgirls know that I'm hers— The customer in this room is the property of Landman. Hands off.

To tell you the truth, the dress was a little tight. I could hardly get into it, no matter how I held in and no matter how Landman's nimble fingers zipped me up, lest she should lose a sale. I walked out of the dressing room to show Harold.

"I love it."

"Really, Harold?" (He was no judge, you know. Harold was loving everything these days.)

"It looks great."

"It's too tight, I can't breathe."

"So?"

"Whadda you mean, 'so'?"

"Whadda you have to breathe for?"

He was right—absolutely right. Who needs to breathe in a grave. And so what if I gain a few pounds? Let them pin it up the back. Mrs. Landman, wrap it up!

My mother's gonna faint when she sees the dress. Did you faint, Mom? I left the price tag on. They're all gonna faint. Sheila Levine will be the hit of the funeral.

Did you ever buy good underwear? I mean really good underwear? Up until now, good underwear meant stuff without holes, still had the elastic in, wasn't stained from my period. I can't tell you how many perfectly good underpants I have ruined at "that time of the month"—Super Tampax or not.

I wanted to buy really good underwear. I never had any. When I was a little girl, I had pants with the days of the week on them. And that, no matter how you look at it, cannot be classified as very good underwear. Then it was Carter's sixteen-year-old (when I was twelve). The Lollipop pants, every color of the rainbow. And, finally, bikini underwear—stomach hanging over—eighty-nine cents to two dollars a pair, never more, never less. Yes, I bought underwear by rote.

My old roommate Kate did not. She had beige lace everything. It was usually dirty, but it started out being great. I shudder to think of what I was wearing under my clothes at times. If I passed out and they had to take me to the emergency ward, two days out of four I would have been embarrassed about my underwear. Once at camp, I dyed my underpants lavender instead of washing them.

So when I wanted to buy really good underwear, like the stuff Kate's was made of, I couldn't find it. Maybe it's because I had an image in my mind—something embroidered, like Kate's.

Harold, being very patient (all good things come to those who wait), followed me from store to store, up the avenue, looking for the lovelies. One store had some light blue and pink silk, but it wasn't right. I settled. I will be found wearing my robe, very pretty, floor-length, so why buy a new one? Under my robe—are you ready?—light blue . . . no, more of a turquoise, pink lace trim, matching bra, matching slip. Don't ask why a slip under a robe. I just had to—it looked great —the whole thing over thirty-five dollars. Tailored Woman.

Harold and I were both tired, so we will look for the wig another day. You'll die when you see the underwear, the dress. Can't wait to wear them.

You know, there are a lot of ways for one to do away with one's self. I always thought in terms of pills. That seemed neatest. They were the easiest to get. Guns were messy. What do I know about guns? Nobody in my immediate family had ever touched a gun. For that matter, what do I know about ropes? Razor blades? . . . Maybe . . . I don't know . . . I use an electric razor. Pills seem the safest way to do it.

Of course, there are dramatic ways, like jumping. I really don't mind jumping. It's the crashing I would hate. And jump from where? I worked on the second floor and I live on the third floor. I mean, you can't just go into a strange office or apartment and ask to use the ledge. "Excuse me, would you mind if I used your ledge for a minute?" Nah. And did you ever try to climb out on a ledge? It's practically impossible. The windows aren't wide enough to get out, and the ledges are really not wide enough to stand on.

A bridge? No. I want them to find me and bury me in that great dress. I don't want them to have to drag the river and have to bury me all pruney-looking and green. That's no way to wow them at a funeral.

Of course there's the chicken's way of committing suicide. Like I could take a walk along Riverside Drive at night. That would do it. Or I could get on the BMT and ride to Brooklyn alone at about 3 A.M. That would do it. Or I could leave my door unlocked one night. Living in Manhattan really has its advantages.

Or I could go to one of the campus riots and piss off the National Guard. That would do it.

Or I could march for peace and get beaten to death.

I think pills. Harold thinks pills, too.

Dear, sweet Harold, so considerate. He thought pills because he thought it would hurt me least. Is that considerate? I ask you. Are those the thoughts of one hell-of-a-considerate-person?

Another question. How do you do it with pills? I mean really do it. If only Marilyn Monroe were alive today. You don't just ask a doctor for a prescription for poison pills. What I did was to go to my neighborhood drugstore. You wanna die, you go to your neighborhood drugstore.

(Me) "Excuse me, could you please tell me where the sleeping pills are?"

(My neighborhood druggist) "Two aisles down on your right."

Naturally, his directions were of no help (are they ever?), but I managed to find them. Picked the bottle with the largest warning on it. After all, I was not interested in taking a little nap. Back to my neighborhood druggist for a friendly neighborhood chat about suicide.

(Me) "Excuse me, but how many of these would kill a person?" (Holding up the bottle)

(My neighborhood druggist, earnestly looking at bottle) "Those won't kill anybody."

(Me) "Are these the strongest ones you have?"

(My neighborhood druggist, being so earnest and friendly that he walks two aisles down and to his right with me. He picks up another bottle.) "These are the strongest. That is, the strongest that you can buy without a prescription."

(Me, smiling) "And how many of these would kill a person?"

(My N.D.) "Those won't kill anybody."

(Me) "I'm looking for something in a lethal sleeping pill."

(My N.D.) "How come? You're not gonna kill yourself, are ya?"

(Me) "Oh, no, of course not. I'm doing a term paper on sleeping pills."

(My N.D.) "You look too old to be a student."

(Me) "Yes. Listen, do you have anything lethal or not?"

(My N.D.) "Nah, the most any of these will do is put you to sleep for a couple of days and you'll wake up with a headache."

I bought a bottle of Sleep-Eze because I didn't want a scene from my neighborhood druggist. You know how they get when you don't buy.

Harold came through. He got me a whole bottle of black market sleeping pills, Nembutal, I think (they're red), as a going-away present. He had some trouble because there just wasn't anything good around. Either they weren't manufacturing as many pills or suicide is all the rage this season. I'm in.

I ordered the casket—not too expensive but not the cheapest that they have either. The interior is light blue, which goes nicely with the dress. I would have preferred something wilder, but all they had was pastels. The light blue goes.

I also got the wig. It's not fake anything—it's real Dynel . . . long and blond, just like I've always wanted, and only $39.95 at Macy's. Things are falling into place nicely. Today is June 27, a Thursday. July 3 is next Wednesday. Harold is whistling now. He's skipping around the place, sneaking up behind me and doing cute things like pinching my ass and kissing the back of my neck. He adores me. I told him I was going to arrange for my will, and he almost jumped for joy, not because he thinks I'm going to leave him millions—he knows I don't have anything. He's jumping because I'm making things so final.

My will. I never knew that getting a will was so complicated. Whatever happened to all those lawyers in all those old movies who went to the bedside of some rich old man and got everything into order? And where are they now?

Beautiful Ivan, Linda's ex (the world is actually filled with Linda's exes), was the only lawyer I really knew well. I knew friends of my father's who were the greatest lawyers in the country, but I could hardly use one of them now, could I?

I tried an old number of Ivan's . . .

"Hello." (Luck. It was Ivan)

"Hello, Ivan, this is Sheila Levine, Linda Minsk's old roommate." (Does that mean I'm an *old* roommate?)

"Oh, yes, how's Linda?" (He would.)

"She's fine, I guess. She's somewhere in Europe last I heard."

"Oh. Well, what can I do for you . . . uh. . . ." (He forgot my name.)

"Sheila. Ivan, I need a lawyer. I know it's silly, and I'll probably never need it or anything, but I'd like to have a will made up."

207

"I don't do that sort of thing. You know, I'm with Legal Aid now."

"Well, do you know anybody who does that sort of thing? I wouldn't bother you, Ivan, but it's pretty important. I was reading this magazine article that said everybody should have a will."

"Let me give you the number of a friend of mine. He's in private practice. He'll probably be able to help you. [Pause] Here. Barry Hart. 555-2900."

"Thank you. Thank you very much, Ivan."

"You're welcome. 'Bye now."

"Just one more thing, Ivan. The reason I need a will done is because I'm committing suicide, which I wouldn't commit if you would marry me." (I said that —after he had hung up.)

555-2900.

"Hello. Young, Hart, Lang and Huntington."

"I would like to speak with Mr. Hart, please."

"I'm sorry, he's out of town until July twenty-sixth."

"Are Huntington or Young or Lang any good?"

Huntington would see me tomorrow.

And I went tomorrow, which was yesterday, and you wouldn't believe the aggravation I got from him.

(Huntington, without looking at me) "I understand you are interested in having a will. Everyone should." (He was young and dared to wear long sideburns in the law world.)

"Yes."

"All right, your full legal name, date of birth . . ." (We went on with those questions for a while.)

"Mr. Huntington, will this be ready by July third for me to sign or whatever I have to do with it?"

"I doubt it. We'll have it for you right after the July Fourth weekend."

"Well, I need it before. I really do. To be quite frank, Mr. Huntington, I don't expect to live past the weekend."

"Why not?"

"I'm psychic."

"I'll try. You can sign it on Monday."

"Thank you."

"Now, who will be your beneficiary?"

"Do you mean who do I want to leave my things to?"

"Yes, Miss Levine."

"Oh, to a lot of different people. I have a list."

"You mean you don't have one person in mind?"

"No. A lot of different people. I have a list." He looked at me as if I were crazy, which indeed I am.)

Poor Mr. Huntington, sporting sideburns and so upset that I had a list.

"Miss Levine, who is your next of kin?"

"My mother and my father are my next of kin."

"And don't you want to leave everything to them?"

"No."

"I see. Well, this will get a bit more complicated. I'll call my secretary in and you can dictate your list to her."

"Thank you."

And what, I ask you, happened to the days when a great aunt left a favorite niece a watch? This lawyer person was so upset that I had a list.

My will? So what did I have to leave? Less than a monk. I, Sheila Levine, being of sound mind, leave:

Mr. and Mrs. Manny Levine my television set for the bedroom and the knowledge that I did what I wanted to do. They shouldn't feel guilty.

To my roommate, Linda Minsk, my Christian Dior scarf, my Pucci perfume, my Rudi slacks (never worn because they never fit) and my YSL earrings.

To Barbra Streisand, my makeup mirror because she didn't have her nose done either.

To Joshua, alias Alan Goldstein, the chartreuse couch and all the suede I have.

To Norman Berkowitz, you bastard, an eleven-by-fifteen picture of me—it's in the top drawer of my desk. I would like to request that Norman, the bastard, keep the picture of me in his bedroom, prominently displayed at all times . . . and all my unpaid bills.

To Melissa Hinkle, my married sister, my books on child psychology, she shouldn't screw up her daughter's psyche.

To Jennifer Hinkle, my niece, my dishes, silverware and linens—to use when she has her own apartment, provided it's anywhere but New York.

To Rose Lehman's sister, Fran, my typewriter and thank you for getting me my first job.

To Charles Miller, all my "name" shopping bags.

To Will Fisher, I leave nothing. I gave him my virginity, and I think that's enough of a gift.

To Miss Burke from the employment agency, I leave all the dirty clothes in my hamper.

To women's lib, I leave a donation of one hundred dollars in the hopes they use it to make a world where a girl can be single *and* happy. (Sorry it isn't more, girls.)

To Thomas Brown, I leave my diaphragm. Go find some girl in Friday's that it fits.

To Harold Feinberg, I leave all my records, one for each climax.

To the rest of the world, I leave these words: Fuck off.

"Harold?"

"Yes?"

"I made out a will today."

"Yeah."

"Now listen carefully, Harold. It's going to be with a

lawyer named Huntington, James Huntington, at a firm called Young, Hart, Lang and Huntington."

"Come to bed."

"Come on, Harold, this is important." (And I wasn't having climaxes anymore anyway.)

"Their phone number is 555-2900."

"Come to bed." (And he dragged me down.)

"Harold, please. Will you remember about the will?"

"Yes, I'll remember. Now come on, Sheila. Shut up and fuck."

And I had a climax. Another present. Boy, was he being generous lately.

Harold isn't going to save me, you know. Harold is not going to beg me to change my mind or call the police or ambulance or anything. Harold is as excited as I am about the whole thing.

July 2. Let me sort it all out. Sex with Harold has been fantastic. No one has ever had such a great send-off. And no diaphragms. Heaven on earth.

I ordered the flowers. One huge bouquet—twenty three fifty, it cost me. Long-stemmed white roses and the card reads, "To Sheila, I'm sorry I killed you. It was out of love. If only you would have agreed to marry me, I wouldn't have done it. Love, Norm." Now, I didn't say it was Norman and there's no way that he can get into real trouble, but let him sweat it out. A little investigation maybe.

I spoke to Rabbi Stine. Does he have a eulogy for me! He talks about vaginal spray and everything. He's gonna say how it's such a shame that a girl feels she has to be married and how we should teach our daughters to be human beings as well as wives. And how every person there is responsible for my death. Very dramatic.

And Rabbi Stine is going to suggest that no one send flowers. In lieu of flowers, send money to the Sheila

Levine Memorial Fund. And I suggested that the money be used for a scholarship for a girl who wants to go to college, but not to the School of Education, like her mother wants her to.

My obituary. Harold has a copy to send to the New York *Times* immediately. "Died. Sheila Levine, 31. Graduate of NYU Department of Dramatic Arts. Secretary for Mr. Frank Holland, taught at Jr. High 71. Died because she wasn't married. Is survived by her mother and father." So do you think they'll print it?

I even have a picture to go with the obituary, should any of the papers request it. I went into a regular photographer on Eighth Street. Just a regular photographer with lots of Bar Mitzvah boys and brides in the window. So I sit down to have my picture taken and I'm trying to look very dignified just in case the New York *Times* wants to print it, and the photographer is doing anything he can, short of dropping his pants, to get me to smile.

"Miss, I'm not going to get a good picture of you unless you smile."

"You don't understand. I don't want a smiley picture."

"What do you want it for, an obituary?" (And I smiled and he took the picture.)

Mom, Dad, listen. There are so many last-minute things. People are going to send sympathy cards and letters. And you're going to have to answer them. What can I say? Please write back: Thank you very much for your expression of sympathy. Our daughter, Sheila, wanted you to know that you should think twice next time you ask a single girl when she's going to get married.

Harold's bugging me to come to bed, and why not?

Harold just left.
(After fucking) "Sheila?"

"Yeah."

"Sheila, I was invited to go to East Hampton over the fourth."

"That's nice."

"You mean you don't mind?"

"Mind what?"

"That I miss the funeral and everything."

"Whadda you mean miss the funeral?"

"Well, this friend of mine, you know him, we were over there last New Year's Eve, invited me out and asked me to drive out on the afternoon of the third and I said, yes, sort of."

"You said yes?"

"I didn't think you'd mind."

"Wouldn't mind? Harold the fourth is the day of the funeral, or have you forgotten?"

"I haven't forgotten. I just didn't think you'd mind. That's all."

"Well, I do mind."

"I don't see why. You're not going to know who's going to be at your funeral anyway."

"How do you know I won't? Maybe I will know! Maybe I'll be looking down at the whole thing and laughing. Laughing at you, Harold!"

"It's not every day I get invited to the Hamptons!"

"So go. Why don't you go now, Harold? I never want to see you again." (Never, never in my whole life. And he went.)

"Hello, is this Mr. Huntington's secretary? I'd like to make a teeny-tiny change in my will. I'd like to leave a guy named Harold out of it."

July 3. It's tomorrow. Last night was my Farewell to Life night, and I want you all to know I slept very well. Extremely well, thank you. No lying awake wondering if I'm doing the right thing. Actually, I have only two things to worry about now: afterlife and reincarnation. If there is such a thing as reincarnation and I come back in another life, please, God, I'd rather be a frog than a single girl again. And suppose I end up in hell? It should be nice compared to living in Manhattan. There's probably a lot of single girls down there, in the suicide section alone.

Everything is done. The apartment is clean. New underwear is on. The clothes for the funeral are all laid out. My magazine subscriptions are all canceled, my rent is paid, and my telephone service goes off the end of the month. My plot is ready, casket bought, tombstone engraved. Harold hasn't had a change of heart, and he's not worth living for anyway. Everything in order and YES . . . I'VE TAKEN THE PILLS, every one of the little red devils in the bottle.

I don't feel a thing yet. Do you ever remember hearing in high school about this scientist who gave himself poison and was going to record what was happening to him for the sake of science. Remember him? Here's Sheila Levine at the typewriter waiting to feel something and not feeling a goddamn thing. Like that scientist, didn't we hear about him in biology, Madeline? Anyway, I heard that he put dots on the paper when it was starting to affect him. ONLY IT AIN'T AFFECTING ME! I'm gonna put dots on the paper, and when the dots stop, you know Sheila's gone.

Here come the dots. ....
....
....
....
....
....
....
....
....
....

....
....
....
....
....
....
....
...............................Shit! I don't feel a thing............
....
....
....
....
...............................Oh, hell, it's not working.
The fucking pills are not working, and I don't feel a
thing. Fuck.

Epilogue

NOT MANY PEOPLE get to write an epilogue to their suicide notes. Yeah, yeah, they pumped my stomach. I bet Doris Day never had to have her stomach pumped.

I remember the whole thing as if it were yesterday— it was two days ago. I did finally get drowsy. I lay down on the bed, remembering to cross my legs in a ladylike manner, awaiting the angel of death to tap me on the shoulder and carry me in his arms to the pearly gates. I don't know how much time passed when the knocking on my apartment door started. I heard the knocking, the pounding, the ringing of the doorbell, but I didn't have the strength to move. I had entered the Twilight Zone.

The next thing I remember is the door falling in. It didn't fall like in a James Bond movie or anything. Somebody removed the hinges or something. It's going be be a hell of a problem putting it back in place. All of a sudden I had more men than I have ever had in my apartment at one time. Emergency Squad people, I think. If I ever throw a party again and there are more women than men, I'm definitely going to call the Emergency Squad. They send over an awful lot of men at once. At least three of them moved me to a stretcher. I crossed my legs again.

Well, needless to say, I was very weak but not too weak to be embarrassed by the young couple, obviously in love, who got on the elevator and looked down at me. They really should have express elevators for suicide cases. And I wasn't too weak to ask one of my stretcher-bearers, "How . . . how'd you know?"

"Your mother tried calling you. When you didn't answer, she got nervous and called us. She had a feeling there was something wrong." My psychic-witch mother interfered with my life and my death.

I remember being carried out of the elevator, those poor men and their poor backs. I remember tipping the doorman on my way out of the building. I did. I had a quarter in the pocket of my robe and I gave it to him. I remember being carried into the ambulance. I was placed on the sidewalk for a moment while the doors to the ambulance were being opened. I attracted a small crowd. Every one of them had an unhappy face. All the happy faces in New York go away for the July Fourth weekend.

I must have blacked out in the ambulance. I don't remember entering the hospital or anything. I have no idea what they actually did to me. Whatever they did, they ripped my good underwear. The next thing I knew, I was in heaven. If you opened your eyes and saw Warren Beatty and five of his good-looking friends, where would you think you were? I thought, "So, this is it. Sheila, you made it—heaven. What they probably do here is grant you one wish and they sure as hell knew what mine was."

I heard voices talking about how I was coming to, and I kept thinking, "Coming to what?" Warren Beatty came in closer, like he was going to kiss me, only he didn't. I couldn't figure out what was happening.

The total confusion lasted several minutes and then. "Sheila, darling, are you all right, my baby?"

Therre was that voice, the same voice that told me I had to wear a sweater over my Halloween costume. That voice brought me back to reality immediately.

217

Dr. Warren Beatty and his friends turned into interns, and heaven was a hospital room at Bellevue.

My mother was completely irrational about the whole thing. She couldn't understand how an entire bottle of sleeping pills accidentally got into my stomach. My father said nothing, as usual.

Henry Rossman and Rabbi Stine were very ticked off at me. Rossman was upset because I canceled the plot and because I lied to him. He said in his thirty-six years of being a funeral director, nobody had ever canceled a plot. He was crushed, but not as crushed as the good rabbi. He didn't call, but his secretary did. She traced me down by calling Rossman's. Did I get it from the rabbi's secretary. How dare I waste the rabbi's time with a fake suicide. The rabbi is very busy you know.

Everyone kept telling me to cheer up, and I did. Not because they told me to. It was Dr. Warren Beatty and his intern friends who finally did the job. They were around all the time, just checking things. (They had me on the intravenous thing—water with sugar. Just what I needed being pushed through the body, right?) Yeah, it was those men in the white coats that made me want to live. They're all attractive, and they're all concerned, or seem to be. They smile at me. All I need is one out of the six.

I'm going back to my apartment. (I'll convert the casket into a couch.) I'm going to get a new job. I'm older than the employment agency ladies now. Maybe they'll listen out of respect. Maybe I'll change my name to Ms. Levine. Maybe I'll write an article for *Reader's Digest*—"I Am Sheila's Dead Body."

In about five minutes one of those medical men will be in here poking around. Look, you never know when one of them is going to come in, check the bedpan and propose. You wanna know something? Mom, Dad, Rabbi, listen. I don't want to die. I want to date! I hope to God somebody put the door back on my apartment.

ABOUT THE AUTHOR

GAIL PARENT, like her heroine, attended Syracuse before receiving a degree from New York University. Unlike her heroine, she married one week after graduation and now lives with her husband, Lair, and their two sons, Kevin and Gregory, in Los Angeles. Gail and her partner, Kenny Solms, are two of the most successful young writers in Hollywood. They wrote the *Carol Burnett Show* for four years, and their numerous other credits include television specials, situation comedies and movies for television. They are presently writing a screenplay for Ross Hunter, as well as a Broadway musical. *SHEILA LEVINE IS DEAD AND LIVING IN NEW YORK* is Gail Parent's first novel.

RELAX!
SIT DOWN
and Catch Up On Your Reading!

☐	THE MONEYCHANGERS by Arthur Hailey	(2300—$1.95)
☐	THE GREAT TRAIN ROBBERY by Michael Crichton	(2424—$1.95)
☐	THE EAGLE HAS LANDED by Jack Higgins	(2500—$1.95)
☐	RAGTIME by E. L. Doctorow	(2600—$2.25)
☐	CONFLICT OF INTEREST by Les Whitten	(10360—$1.95)
☐	THE SWISS ACCOUNT by Leslie Waller	(10092—$1.95)
☐	THE ODESSA FILE by Frederick Forsyth	(2964—$1.95)
☐	ONCE IS NOT ENOUGH by Jacqueline Susann	(8000—$1.95)
☐	JAWS by Peter Benchley	(8500—$1.95)
☐	TINKER, TAILOR, SOLDIER, SPY by John Le Carre	(8844—$1.95)
☐	THE DOGS OF WAR by Frederick Forsyth	(8884—$1.95)
☐	THE R DOCUMENT by Irving Wallace	(10090—$2.25)
☐	MAVREEN by Claire Lorrimer	(10208—$1.95)
☐	THE HARRAD EXPERIMENT by Robert Rimmer	(10357—$1.95)
☐	THE DEEP by Peter Benchley	(10422—$2.25)
☐	DOLORES by Jacqueline Susann	(10500—$1.95)
☐	THE LOVE MACHINE by Jacqueline Susann	(11601—$2.25)
☐	BURR by Gore Vidal	(10600—$2.25)
☐	THE DAY OF THE JACKAL by Frederick Forsyth	(10857—$1.95)
☐	BLACK SUNDAY by Thomas Harris	(10940—$2.25)
☐	PROVINCETOWN by Burt Hirschfield	(11057—$1.95)
☐	THE BEGGARS ARE COMING by Mary Loos	(11330—$1.95)

Buy them at your local bookstore or use this handy coupon for ordering:

Bantam Books, Inc., Dept. FBB, 414 East Golf Road, Des Plaines, Ill. 60016

Please send me the books I have checked above. I am enclosing $_____
(please add 50¢ to cover postage and handling). Send check or money order
—no cash or C.O.D.'s please.

Mr/Mrs/Miss_____

Address_____

City_____State/Zip_____

FBB—12/77

Please allow four weeks for delivery. This offer expires 6/78.
